THE IDEAL VICTIM

Gillean Campbell

Copyright Notice

Dedication

To **Lisa and Sandy,**

The best friends I could have ever wished for. I'm grateful to have you both in my life.

Table of Contents

PROLOGUE

Justine Maxwell opened her dark blue eyes and tried to blink away the fog that enveloped her mind. She felt like her body weighed two tons, and she had a pounding headache. Justine remembered that she'd started driving home, but she couldn't remember arriving. Justine turned her head and saw that she was in a small room without any windows. She was laying on a cold concrete floor next to one of the room's cinderblock walls. Justine tried to sit up, but her body wouldn't cooperate. She closed her eyes and fell back to sleep. When Justine opened her eyes a second time, she saw a glass of water sitting on the floor beside her. Her mouth was so dry that she drank the contents without stopping. When Justine realized that someone had been in the room while she slept, fear crept in and seized the space that confusion had previously occupied.

Now that she could move, Justine pushed herself into a sitting position and surveyed the room. An industrial light hung in the center of the ceiling, but the minor amount of illumination it provided did little to dispel the gloom. Justine saw that there was an old-fashioned white porcelain toilet and sink in the opposite corner. Above the toilet, a shower head stuck out of the wall at a ninety degree angle. She could hear the slow plop, plop, plop of the dripping water as it hit the toilet seat. A roll of toilet paper sat on the floor. Next to the sink, one white bath towel and one white hand towel hung from a rack attached to the wall. Other than that, the room looked empty.

Justine stood and slowly made her way around the entire room, running her hands up and down the walls as she went. Then, she got down on her hands and knees and crawled around the room, moving her hands back and forth across the floor. Justine didn't find anything besides a small drain for the shower. She decided that the light must be controlled from outside of the room because there were no switches inside. Justine ran her hands over the flat-panel steel door. The handle didn't budge when she tried to turn it. Justine stood still for a few seconds and listened. She pressed her ear against the cold metal. Justine couldn't hear any sound from outside the room.

The cold was beginning to make Justine shiver. She sat in the corner again and wrapped her arms around her legs. She sat like that until her entire body began to shake. Justine pulled her arms out of her shirt and put them on the inside of it. She hugged herself. The warmth of her torso felt nice against her cold arms. Justine laid her forehead on her knees and closed her eyes.

After what seemed like hours, the metal door swung inward with a loud screech. Justine jumped to her feet, pushing herself as far as possible into the corner. A man wearing blue jeans and a long sleeved black shirt came into the room. He turned and *closed and locked the door behind him. The man shoved the key into a front pocket and turned to Justine. A burlap sack covered his head and neck. There were small holes where the man's eyes and mouth were. He reminded Justine of a scarecrow.*

Justine's voice quivered as she asked, "Who are you and what do you want?"

The man stepped toward Justine. His words were distorted by the sack over his head. "I want to get to know you better."

Justine completely forgot about being cold. She tried to get further away from the man, but her back was already against the wall. Unconsciously, Justine started to side-step to the right.

"Justine, listen to me. These are the rules. If you're good, I'll reward you. If you're not, I'll punish you. Now, I want you to stop trying to get away from me." He motioned with his hand around the room. "There's nowhere to go."

Justine felt her heart hammer in her chest. Panic set in, and she started to run.

The man yelled. "Justine. Stop!!" He quickly closed the distance to where Justine had frozen in place. The man slapped her so hard that she fell sideways. Justine's head slammed into the cinderblock wall, and she toppled to her hands and knees. He grabbed her by the hair, forcing her to lie on her back. Justine screamed, and the man slapped her again. Tears streamed out of

6

Justine's eyes and fell onto her long blonde hair. The man straddled her legs, pinning them to the ground. Justine swatted ineffectually at his head. He backhanded her. Justine covered her face with her hands and sobbed. "Stop. I'll be good. Please, stop."

The man stood and looked down at her. "Do you understand the rules?"

Justine nodded and continued to cry.

"Get up."

Justine rolled onto her side and pushed herself first onto her hands and knees, then onto her feet. Eyes downcast, Justine watched as her tears wet the concrete floor.

"You control whether I hurt you or not. If you obey me, I won't have to hurt you. Understand?"

Justine nodded.

"I didn't hear you."

Justine stammered. "Yes... yes."

"Good."

CHAPTER 1

Sheriff's Detective Dani McKenna sat at her office desk in Kalispell, Montana. Her eyebrows were drawn together in a scowl as her fingers tapped on the keyboard of her computer.

Corporal Lenny Tirrell stomped into the office Dani shared with Detective Cliff Powers. "McKenna! Why don't I have that burglary report on my desk?!" Tirrell growled.

"I'm working on it right now, sir."

"Well, I want it by COB today! Is that clear?"

"Crystal, sir."

"Every dang time," Tirrell mumbled as he stormed out of the room shaking his head, jowls jiggling.

The corners of Powers' caramel colored eyes crinkled as he started chuckling.

"Bite me," Dani said, leaning back in her chair. "I love this job, but I hate the paperwork that comes with it."

"I know. You've told me that a thousand times."

"Can't we at least take turns writing up the reports?"

"As I've told you a thousand times…" Powers said, emphasizing the word 'you'. "…the junior detective does the paperwork. I had to do it when I was junior. Everyone did. So, get over it."

"Well. The junior detective is supposed to drive the senior detective around too. And, you never let me drive."

"I like to drive."

"Uh huh. I rest my point."

Powers tipped his head toward the ceiling and laughed. "Touché."

Dani's and Powers' gray metal desks sat face-to-face on the right side of the office. Dani's faced the door, while Powers' faced the window. A matching set of desks sat four feet away, leaving a corridor between the two pairs. Each held a corded speakerphone with caller identification and a laptop. The only other things on Dani's desktop were a black inked pen, a yellow highlighter, and a legal pad. These were all lying to the right of her computer. The bottom of the legal pad was perfectly aligned with the edge of the desktop. In contrast, Powers' desk was littered with so much paper that the top was almost invisible.

The Detective Division's compact secretary shuffled into the room and over to Dani. "A kid dropped this off for you," Connie Sams said, holding out a manila envelope.

Dani looked up, confused. She'd never received mail at the office before. Taking the envelope, she asked, "What's in it?"

"I don't know. I didn't look." Exiting the way she'd come, Connie's shoes made a chirping sound as she shuffled across the linoleum floor.

Dani probed the envelope with her fingers, trying to determine what was inside. Feeling nothing, she flipped it around, looking first at the back, then at the front. No address. No markings. 'Detective Dani McKenna. PERSONAL' was hand printed on the front in large, black letters. Dani carefully tore the top of the envelope. She squeezed the sides, causing it to open. Peering inside, Dani saw that there was nothing but a piece of typing paper. She grasped the right top corner of the paper between her thumb and index finger and slid it out of the envelope. Dani flipped the paper front and back, then grasped the other top corner in the same manner.

"Well? What the hell does it say?" Powers asked, leaning forward on his chair.

Dani read aloud. "Dearest Dani, The Bible says 'Cursed is the one who is slack in doing the Lord's work. Cursed is the one who holds back his sword from shedding blood.' The Lord says 'I will send the sword to kill. In your hills, and in your valleys, and in all your rivers, shall they fall that are slain with the sword.' I am the

Lord's sword, and I will not hold back. I look forward to talking to you again soon. Love, Michael."

"So. This guy's what? The archangel?" Powers asked, rolling his deep set eyes.

Dani dropped the note on top of the envelope and rushed out of the room.

"Where the hell are you going?!" Powers yelled.

Dani raced down the hall to Connie's desk. "Where did that kid go?"

"He left." Connie pointed. "Out the front doors."

"Boy or girl?"

"Boy."

"What was he wearing?"

"Jeans and a red sweatshirt, I think. Is somethin' wrong?" Connie asked as Dani sprinted away.

Dani raced out onto the front sidewalk and looked both ways. She didn't see the boy. Dani turned to her right and started running on the sidewalk along Main Street. She looked for the boy between the cars parked in the Flathead County Justice Center's open air lot. When she reached the next cross street,

Dani looked both ways again, turned to her right, and continued to run.

People driving by slowed to look at the woman with a handgun on her hip sprinting down the sidewalk.

Dani continued to run in a circular direction around the Center. She also looked for the boy between the trees and buildings on the opposite side of the street. There was no sign of him anywhere. Dani stopped and placed her hands on her hips, taking deep breaths, trying to calm her racing heart. Blue eyes flashing, she mumbled, "Where did you go?"

As Dani approached the front of the building again, she saw Powers standing in the doorway. Tall and burly with buzzed dark brown hair, he was hard to miss. When Dani got closer, she saw that Powers was running his hand back and forth over his hair. An unconscious habit of his. "Anything?" he asked.

Dani shook her head and surged through the front doors with Powers trailing behind.

Deputy County Attorney Tate Howland stood in the building's central entryway. The County Attorney and his deputies were located on the second floor of the Justice Center. Tate's chiseled face showed his concern. "Hey. Everything okay?" he asked Dani. "I saw you running outside."

"Fine," Dani said as she passed Tate. Without stopping, she finger combed her long honey blonde hair, securing it in the low ponytail that she always wore at work.

Powers gave Howland a friendly slap on the back. "Dani got a note from some freak."

Howland looked at Dani's retreating form, then back at Powers. "Threatening?" he asked.

"Not sure yet. Quoting the Bible."

"I don't like the sound of that," Howland said.

"She can take care of herself. And, she sure wouldn't like us acting like she can't."

"I know. But I still don't have to like it."

Powers patted Tate on the back again and hurried down the hallway after Dani.

Dani sat down at her desk. She removed two clear plastic evidence sheaths from the top drawer. She placed the envelope in one sheath and the typed note in another. "So? What do you make of this?" Dani asked Powers as he strode back into the office.

Powers placed both hands flat on his desk, leaning forward from the hips. "We'd better show this to the boss."

The two walked down the hallway, past Connie's desk, to Tirrell's office. Powers knocked on the frame of the sheriff's office door.

Tirrell motioned them in with a pudgy hand. His heavy lidded gray eyes looked questioningly from Powers to Dani and back.

Dani leaned across Tirrell's well-ordered desk to give him the sleeved note. Tirrell's pot belly kept him from reaching too far forward. Dani said, "Kid delivered it to Connie. No sign of him."

Dani and Powers each sat in one of the two tan upholstered chairs in front of Tirrell's scarred wooden desk.

Light bounced off of the sheriff's receding hairline as he read the note. When he finished, he looked up and asked Dani, "You worried about this?"

"No, sir."

"You know anyone named Michael?"

"Not that I can think of."

Tirrell rubbed his forefinger across the end of his bulbous nose. "Well, nothing we can do unless something actually happens."

~~~

By five that evening Dani had finished her tedious felony burglary report. Two teens had pled guilty to all four counts. She took the paperwork to Tirrell's office.

"About dang time!" Tirrell said as Dani handed him a copy of the report.

"Yes, sir." Dani turned to leave the room.

Tirrell stopped her. "McKenna."

Dani turned back around. "Yes, sir?"

"Just be a little more vigilant tonight. Just in case."

Dani nodded. "I will. Thank you, sir."

Powers was standing at Connie's desk when Dani started back down the hallway to their office.

"I'm sorry, Dani," Connie said as Dani approached her. Connie's u-shaped reception station sat between Tirrell's office and the office the detectives shared.

Dani gave Connie a small smile. "It's okay. No worries."

"I didn't expect it. Somethin' like that happenin' here."

Dani nodded. "Really, don't sweat it, Connie. You couldn't have known."

Powers rapped his knuckles on the top of Connie's desk. "I'm outta here," Powers said. "See you tomorrow."

"Good night," Dani said. Back at her desk, Dani aligned the pen and highlighter parallel to the side of the laptop. Then, she took her oversized, hobo-style, black leather handbag out of her bottom drawer. Dani looked at her desk one more time before she left to assure herself everything was in its place.

Dani drove the short distance to Center Street. She parked in back of the red brick building. The area was somewhat sketchy. The first time Dani had come here, she'd been afraid to get out of the car. After so much time, she didn't give it a thought. Dani took a gym bag out of the back of her Jeep, locked the doors, and walked down the short flight of concrete stairs. She rapped on the dented metal door.

Damian Irvin opened the door to his boxing studio and smiled at Dani. He pulled her into a bear hug, holding her for a few seconds. "How're you doing today?" Irvin was five foot eleven inches of pure muscle. He kept his auburn hair so short that most of his head was skull. Irvin had small brown eyes, a cleft chin, and a mouth that was never far from a smile. The white t-shirt he was wearing stretched tight across his pecs and arms. Irvin locked the door behind Dani.

As usual, Dani could smell the faint odor of sweat inside the large boxing gym. "I'm good. How are you, Damian?"

"I'm well. Ready to work up a sweat?"

"I'll go change. Be back in a sec." Dani went into the small bathroom at the back of the gym and locked the door. She opened the gym bag, removed a tank top, shorts, and tennis shoes, and set them on the side of the sink. As Dani undressed, she put everything in the gym bag. First, she slipped the silver chain of her badge holder over her head. Dani unzipped her black tactical boots and pulled them off. She unbuckled her black leather belt and began pulling it out of the loops of her tan cargo pants. Dani pulled her belt out of the back of the holster that she carried her Glock in. Then, she removed the cell phone carrying case from the belt. Dani took off her pants. She unbuttoned her black blouse and shrugged out of it.

When Dani came out of the bathroom, Irvin was wrapping his wrists. Dani sat on a metal folding chair next to him and began wrapping hers. When she'd finished, Irvin asked, "Ready?" Dani nodded.

The two moved over to the heavy punching bags that were hanging from the ceiling by thick, shiny chains. They warmed up at the bags for thirty minutes. They were both sweating as they inserted their mouth gear. Dani and Irvin squared off against each other on the large mat covered floor. They both assumed a fighting stance with their chins lowered and hands up. Neither wore boxing gloves because these were full contact sparring

17

sessions. Irvin moved toward Dani and threw two punches at her head. Dani moved quickly, using footwork to transport her body. She blocked the blows with her forearms and threw a punch at Irvin's neck. He blocked it. Dani threw a second punch, hitting Irvin on his right temple.

"Good!" Irvin threw a punch, catching Dani in the ribcage. She grunted. Irvin said, "Come on. Concentrate! You're blinking."

The two continued to spar for an hour, trading blows. Blood trickled down Dani's cheek from a small cut above her eye. Her knuckles were also bloody.

Wiping his brow with the hem of his t-shirt, Irvin said, "Okay. That's it for today." The two shook hands.

Irvin had been training Dani to defend herself for the past five years. She had a private session with him once a week.

"Let me clean that cut," Irvin said, pointing at Dani's brow.

"Thanks, Damian, but I'm fine. I'll take care of it at home."

Irvin shrugged. "If you say so. I'll walk you out."

Dani grabbed her gym bag and handbag and walked with Irvin to the door. She said, "See you next Monday."

~~~

Dani's started to relax as she drove the last half-mile on North Ashley Lake Road toward home. When she saw her log house with its forest green trim, Dani sighed and rolled her shoulders. Her forty pound black Schnauzer, Bo, excitedly ran back and forth next to the garage. Before Dani pulled onto the gravel driveway, she reached up to the visor and pushed the button on the garage door opener. The door opened to its full extent as Dani pulled up to it. Dani parked her white Jeep Renegade in the middle of the two-car garage. She pushed the button again on the remote. Dani waited until the door was completely closed before unlocking the Jeep. She picked up her handbag and gym bag from between the two front seats. Dani pushed the lock button on the key fob after getting out. Then, she pushed it again, waiting to hear the blare of the Jeep's horn.

Dani unlocked the doorknob and the deadbolt into the house. She pushed the wooden door open and stepped inside. Dani entered the pass code on the touchpad for her security system and pressed the button for home mode. She relocked the door, and hung her handbag and the keys on hooks next to the door.

Bo had darted back through his dog door in the laundry room and patiently watched this ritual. When Dani turned around, he started wagging his short tail. "Hello, boy. How was your day?" She rubbed Bo's silky ears. He leaned against Dani as if giving her a welcome home hug. "Come on. I'll change, and we can go for a walk."

The two continued through the mudroom into the spacious kitchen. The kitchen was open to the two-story great room beyond. Dani stopped at the refrigerator to make sure that there was a bottle of Chardonnay inside. She headed to the master suite with Bo following like a shadow.

Dani took off her workout clothes. It was fifty-six degrees outside, so she changed into black sweatpants and a gray striped sweatshirt. She removed her badge, gun, and cell phone from the gym bag and set them on the nightstand next to her bed. Dani set her boots on the floor. She took the rest of the clothes into the roomy walk-in closet, and put them in the hamper. Dani moved into the bathroom and gently washed her face in the sink. She applied a butterfly bandage to the cut above her eyebrow, then said, "Let's go."

Bo wagged his tail and sauntered through the living room to the front doors. Dani disarmed the security system from her cell phone. She removed a set of keys from a hook by the doors and opened the two locks. Bo looked into Dani's eyes, waiting for permission to go outside. She released him with one word. "Okay." Bo sprinted through the door. Nose to the ground, he started smelling around the front of the house. Dani followed him out, locked the door, and armed the security system. She walked across the wooden porch and down the stone steps that led to the naturally growing grass surrounding the house. As Dani started walking, Bo came around to her left side and kept pace with her.

There was no need for a leash. Dani had acquired Bo when he was three months old. She'd been twenty-one at the time. The two had been alone together for the past eight years. Early on, Dani had spent many hours training Bo. Now, she felt that he could understand everything she said.

Dani's house was thirteen miles from Kalispell. It sat on two acres of timbered land that was fronted by Ashley Lake. The nearest home was a half-mile down the lake's pebble beach. Dani loved the solitude and quiet afforded by the remoteness.

When Dani and Bo reached the waterfront, she laughed as he frolicked in the cold, clear water. As Bo splashed and played, Dani strolled along the water's edge. Unbidden, the vision of a dark room entered Dani's mind. She stopped and gasped. Bo's head whipped around. Growling deep in his chest, he ran to her side. Dani held up her hand, and Bo quieted. "Good boy," she said, rubbing his head. "Come on. Let's head back."

Inside, Bo headed straight for the kitchen, knowing what was coming next. Dani took his dry food out of a bottom kitchen cabinet and poured it into his bowl. She'd thrown some chicken and vegetables into the crockpot before leaving for work that morning. As Bo ate, Dani spooned the mixture into a bowl and poured herself a glass of wine. Dani waited for Bo to finish eating before she carried her food out to the bistro table on the covered front porch.

As Dani ate and sipped wine, she took in the magnificent view across the lake. The Whitefish Mountain Range rose majestically in the background of the small peninsula that sat a mile away. Dani watched as a harrier hawk glided overhead. Its black wing tips were prominent against cream colored wings. She followed it as it soared in a circle, rising higher and higher. The sun dipped behind the mountains, and shadows gathered in the corners.

The two went back inside the house. Dani locked the door after herself, pulling hard on the knob to make certain it wouldn't open. Then, she built a roaring fire in the floor-to-ceiling stacked stone fireplace. She flipped the switch of the turntable resting on an oak console table and started her favorite jazz record playing.

Dani took her glass of wine to the master bath and filled the tub. She added several cups of lavender salts. Dani removed her clothes and looked at the bruise on her ribs. She carefully probed it and searched her body for more. Dani found another one forming on the outside of her right thigh. With a sigh, she climbed into the soaking tub and lowered herself up to her neck into the hot water. "Aaah. That feels good." Bo sat on the bath rug and put his head on the edge of the bathtub. Dani soaked for fifteen minutes. Then, she pulled herself out of the tub and put on striped terry pajamas and thick socks.

Carrying the wine glass, Dani padded back to the living room. She settled into her favorite oversized armchair in front of the crackling fire. Bo plopped down on the floor beside her chair. Dani sipped wine and listened to the music that always soothed her.

When Dani's cell phone rang, she groaned and pushed herself out of the chair. Dani looked at the caller identification and swiped the answer button on the screen. "Hi, Garrett."

"How's my little sis?"

"I'm doing fine. How are you?"

"Great. How's the detective business going?"

"It's good."

"Still liking hunting down bad guys?"

"Yes. I still like it. How about you? Still like working with your dad?"

"Oh, you know how he is."

"He's an asshole," Dani said.

Garrett chuckled. "He is that."

A few seconds of silence passed before Garrett asked, "Have you talked to your mom?"

"No. And, I'm not going to. So, please stop trying to push me."

"How long are you going to hold a grudge?"

"You have to be kidding me, Garrett." Dani raised her voice a notch. "You're calling it a grudge? You know it's a lot more than that. I can never forgive her for what she did… Or, I should say, didn't do. So, stop… please."

"Okay, okay. I'm sorry, D. I won't ask again. I don't want to fight with you. I called to see how you are and let you know that I love you."

"I love you too. Thanks for checking on me."

When it was time for bed, Dani performed her nightly routine. She checked all of the locks on the doors and windows in the house, and made sure the security system was armed.

CHAPTER 2

Powers strode into the office and over to his desk. He stopped cold when he looked at Dani. Powers perused her face and shook his head. "I don't understand why the hell you do that to yourself week after week. He pointed. "You already have one scar. You trying for more?"

Dani ignored him, changing the subject. "I've been doing some research." She leaned back in her desk chair.

Powers sat at his desk. "Oh yeah? On what?"

"Yesterday's note. Michael strung several verses together from different versions of the bible. In case you're interested, the part about being cursed is Jeremiah 48:10. The second part about sending the sword is Jeremiah 15:3. The last part about where the slain will fall is Ezekiel 35:8." Dani paused. "Also, I looked up the archangel Michael." Dani used her fingers to air quote as she said, "He leads God's armies against Satan's forces."

Powers shrugged. "Anyone could get their hands on all that in a library or on the internet. Like you did."

The detectives heard Connie's shuffling gate as she hurried down the hallway. Entering the office, Connie held up a plain manila envelope by one corner. "This was sittin' on my desk when

25

I came in this morning." She moved to Dani. "I looked, but I didn't see anyone around." Connie looked down at the envelope and up at Dani. "It's marked 'personal' for you again."

Dani and Powers looked at each other. Dani took a pair of latex gloves out of the top drawer of her desk and put them on. She held out her hand for the envelope. "Thanks, Connie. I'll take it." As Dani had the day before, she felt the envelope, looked at both sides, and slit the top open. Dani turned the envelope upside down and shook it. A typed note and two photographs fell onto her desk.

Dani picked up the note first and read it out loud. "Dearest Dani, The Bible says 'You are not to allow a sorceress to live.' Enclosed are photos of the sorceress. I look forward to talking to you again soon. Love, Michael."

Connie rang her hands and said, "Dear Lord. What's goin' on?"

"I sure as hell don't know," Powers said, coming around to Dani's desk. He ran his right hand over his bristly hair.

Connie shook her head and mumbled a prayer as she walked back to her desk.

Dani pulled four evidence sheaths out of her desk drawer. She put the envelope, the note, and the two photographs inside separate sheaths. The two detectives inspected the pictures. One photograph was a close-up of the woman. She had an attractive oval face with high cheekbones, full lips, a straight nose, and cornflower blue

26

eyes. The other photograph was of the same woman, standing on a sidewalk kissing a man. She was tall and slim, with long blonde hair. Dani turned the pictures over. The back of both had 'HP Advanced' printed on them.

Dani rubbed her forehead. "Is this guy for real?"

"I think we have to assume so," Powers said. "Let's show these to the boss. See what he says."

The detectives hustled to Tirrell's office, entering without knocking. Dani handed the sheriff the four sheaths. "The envelope was on Connie's desk when she got in this morning."

Tirrell scrutinized the items. He sat quietly for a long moment, then handed the sheaths back to Dani. "Have Connie get these and the first note couriered over to the state crime lab in Missoula. I'll call Steve Corr, the administrator. Explain the situation and get them made a top priority."

Dani nodded. "We'll start trying to ID the woman." The detectives returned to their office, where Dani made copies of the two notes and the photographs.

Powers held out his hand. "I'll take the originals to Connie."

Dani enlarged the pictures until each one fit on a standard sized sheet of paper. Dani taped one set of the copies on a whiteboard that was stored against one wall of the office. She wheeled the whiteboard over to her desk and angled it so that Powers could see it from his desk too. At the large white copier that sat in a corner, she scanned the close-up photograph of the woman.

Powers came back into the office. "They'll be at the lab in an hour. I figure we should hear back sometime tomorrow."

"I scanned the photo of the woman," Dani said. "We should run it through the facial recognition system and see if she was ever arrested. If she was, we could ID her that way."

"I'll do it." Powers sat and tapped the keys on his computer's keyboard. "It's running."

Dani stared at the copies of the photographs. Powers came over and stood next to Dani in front of the whiteboard. Dani tapped the picture of the woman kissing the man. "What's this building they're standing in front of?" She took a magnifying glass out of her desk drawer and held it up to the copy of the photograph. "Big windows. What's that inside the window?" Both Dani and Powell leaned closer.

"There are a couple of tables and chairs," Powers said, pointing. "Not sure what that darker thing is." He squinted, trying to bring the image into focus.

"It looks like a bar to me," Dani said. "This is a hotel." She tapped the picture. "See? This looks like a hotel lobby. All bright and shiny."

28

"Yeah. Could be."

Dani sat at her desk and started typing on her computer. "Let's see if we can find a picture of a hotel in town that matches that photo." Dani typed and clicked for several minutes. Powers leaned on her desk with one hand and looked over her shoulder. "There," Dani said. She compared the photograph of the couple kissing to the image of the hotel on her laptop. "It's the Hilton right down Main Street."

"You're right. It is."

Powers' computer emitted a dinging sound. "Search is done." Powers went around to his desk and sat in front of the computer. He looked at the screen. "No dice. Of course. Would have been too easy if she was in here."

"Let's get over to the Hilton and see if anyone can ID these two."

Dani and Powers both put on their jackets. Dani stuck a copy of the photographs inside her handbag. Powers folded his copies and put them in a pocket of his coat. They stopped by Tirrell's office and told him where they were going and why.

The sheriff's nodded. "Let's just hope this whole thing's a hoax."

"Yes, sir," Powers said. The detectives rushed out of the building and to their assigned vehicle.

Looking out of his office window, Tate Howland watched Dani as she and Powers got into their white Dodge SUV. Howland continued watching until he could no longer see the logo on the side of the vehicle.

The hotel was only five minutes from the Justice Center. When Powers pulled up in front, Dani took the copies of the photographs out of her handbag. "This is it." She held the picture up so that they both could look at it. Powers shook his head in agreement. He parked directly in front of the entrance.

The hotel lobby was spacious and luxurious. Seating areas were arranged in front of the oversized windows and the fireplace. Beyond the lobby, Dani could see a lodge-style bar area with wide-plank dark wood floors. The bar itself was shaped like a horseshoe. Two large screen televisions had been mounted on the wall at each end of the horseshoe. In the middle was a sculpture of a horse rearing up on its hind legs. The front desk was to the left. A young man dressed in a suit stood behind the counter. The name tag pinned to the pocket of his suit jacket identified him as Brandon.

Dani held up her badge. "Sheriff's Detective McKenna. This is Detective Powers." Dani placed the photograph of the couple kissing on the countertop. "We need to identify these two individuals. Do you recognize them?"

"Yes, ma'am. They've been here several times. I remember them because they always check-in during the day and leave a couple of hours later."

The two detectives glanced at each other. Powers raised an eyebrow.

"Do you know their names?" Dani asked. "They're not in any trouble. We just need to speak with them."

Brandon glanced around. "I'm not supposed to give out the names of our guests."

"The woman could be in danger, Brandon," Dani said, leaning in. "I promise that nobody will ever know their IDs came from you."

Brandon looked around again, then whispered, "Let me check." He started tapping on the keyboard of the computer in front of him. "I think the last time they were in here was Thursday or Friday. Yeah. Here it is. This past Friday. The man always pays with his credit card. His name's Dayton Cooke. I don't know what her name is. But, I'm assuming it's not Mrs. Cooke." Brandon took one of the hotel cards off of the countertop and wrote on the back of it. "Here's his name and address."

"Thank you, Brandon," Dani said, smiling at him.

Brandon beamed. "Glad I could help."

As they walked back to the entrance, Powers said, "Ol' Brandon never even glanced at me."

"Bull."

"He'll be dreaming about you tonight, guaranteed."

"Bite me, Powers."

Powers chuckled as Dani shook her head in exasperation at him.

In the SUV, Powers entered Dayton Cooke's address into the onboard GPS housed in the center console. "Lives right by the Village Greens Golf Course. Ten minutes away."

Dani buckled her seat belt. "Let's go."

Cooke's house was one of two on a cul-de-sac. Powers drove down the driveway and parked in front of the garage. The concrete sidewalk on the left led to a gabled porch covering the red front door. They could hear a baby crying inside. Powers rang the doorbell. The baby continued to cry. Powers rang the doorbell again and pounded on the door with his fist. When the baby finally stopped crying, Powers rang the bell again.

The woman that finally answered the door had a heart shaped face, black hair, and blood shot brown eyes. She was dressed in pale pink slacks and a matching long sleeved tunic. "Yes?"

"Sheriff's Detectives McKenna and Powers," Dani said. They held up their badges.

The woman looked back and forth between the badges, then back and forth between Dani's and Powers' faces. "Is something wrong?"

"No, ma'am," Powers said.

"Are you Mrs. Cooke?" Dani asked.

"Yes."

Dani and Powers glanced at each other.

"Is your husband home, ma'am?" Powers asked.

"No. He's at work. Why are you looking for him? Is he okay?"

"He's fine," Powers said. "We need to speak with him."

"Where does he work?" Dani asked.

"He works at GMP on Main Street. He's an architect."

"Thank you, ma'am," Powers said.

Mrs. Cooke stood at the front door, watching as the detectives walked back to their vehicle. Her brow was furrowed, confusion showing on her face.

Back inside the SUV, Powers said, "Sure doesn't look anything like the woman Cooke was kissing in that photo."

Dani shook her head. "Sure doesn't."

Powers drove to where Cooke worked. It was less than a mile north of the Justice Center. When the detectives walked through the frosted front doors, they saw that Dayton Cooke was waiting for them. Cooke introduced himself and shook hands with the detectives. "Charlene called and said you were on your way." Dani and Powers introduced themselves.

"Please, come into my office." Cooke led them past the reception area, where a young woman with dimples smiled at them. A metal sign with the letters 'GMP' on it was mounted on the slate wall behind the reception counter.

Cooke's office was four doors down the carpeted hallway, on the left. Cooke closed the door and shut the blinds on the windows that looked out into the hall. There was a framed photograph of Cooke's wife and baby girl sitting on his desk. Cooke didn't invite Dani and Powers to sit. The three remained standing. "What can I do for you, detectives?"

Dani laid the copy of the photograph of Cooke kissing the blonde woman on his desk. She turned it toward him and tapped it with her index finger. "We're looking for this woman."

Dani thought Cooke looked to be in his late thirties. He must be a good fifteen years older than his wife. Cooke was overweight, with a round face. He sported short graying hair and the five o'clock shadow look that was popular with some men.

Cooke removed his black framed glasses, set them on his desk, and rubbed his eyes with his hands. He put his glasses back on. "What do you want?"

Dani held up a hand. "Don't worry. We're not interested in who you have sex with. We need to find the woman in this photo."

"Where the hell did you get that?" Cooke asked, pointing at the photograph.

"That's not relevant," Powers said, raising his voice.

Dani rephrased the question. "Who's this woman and where can we find her?"

Cooke slid onto the chair behind his desk. "Her name's Josie Aiken. She works here, but she didn't come in today. I don't know where she is."

"Was she scheduled to be out today?" Dani asked.

"No. And, I tried to call Josie on her cell phone, but she didn't answer."

"We're going to need that number, her address, and her husband's name," Powers said. "Write 'em down."

Cooke picked up the cell phone sitting on his desk and tapped on the screen. He took a piece of notepaper out of a wooden cube and wrote down the requested information. Cooke handed the piece of paper to Powers.

Powers read what Cooke had written and nodded at Dani. She opened the office door to leave but turned back to Cooke. "Where does Josie's husband work?"

"He teaches math at Glacier High." Cooke paused. "Is Josie okay?" he asked.

"We'll be in touch if we need anything else," Powers said, turning to leave. As they walked by the receptionist, Dani noticed that the woman was no longer smiling. She motioned with her eyes and whispered, "Offices must have thin walls."

Powers entered Josie Aiken's home address into the GPS in the SUV. He backed out of the parking space on the side of GMP's building, tires squealing on the blacktop. "The Aikens live real close to the Cookes," Powers said. "They probably get together for dinner at each other's houses."

When the detectives pulled up, Dani saw a modern two-story house that stood in contrast to the neighbor's ranch-style homes. The Aiken's house had a flat roof and concrete block walls. Dani

36

and Powers followed the sweeping pebble walkway around to the front of the house. Glass stretched from the ground to the roof along the entire front. This allowed for an uninterrupted view of the Stillwater River, which flowed within fifty yards of the house.

Powers rang the doorbell on the side of glass double doors.

"Please be home," Dani murmured.

Powers rang the bell again and pounded on the door.

Dani cupped both hands around her eyes and leaned into the glass. She could see a large open floor plan, with a living room, dining area, and kitchen. Clear, acrylic stairs led up to the second story.

Powers repeated the ringing and pounding.

Dani shook her head. "I don't see anyone inside. Let's go talk to Josie's husband."

The detectives walked back around the house to the SUV. Powers drove as fast as safely possible to the high school. He parked on Wolfpack Way, in front of the main sidewalk that led to the school's front doors. Dani and Powers entered the building and headed for the central office. A plump older woman sitting at a desk looked up at them. "May I help you?"

The two detectives introduced themselves. Dani said, "We need to speak with George Aiken."

The woman looked flustered. "One moment, please." She scurried over to a door on the left. A metal plaque that read 'Principal' was attached to the front. The woman knocked and entered, glancing back at Dani and Powers. She closed the door behind her. A minute later the woman reemerged with a man who said, "I'm Principal Hardy. I understand you wish to speak to Mr. Aiken. May I ask what this is about?"

"I'm afraid we're not at liberty to discuss the details with you," Powers said.

"Mr. Aiken hasn't done anything wrong," Dani said. "We need to speak with him about his wife."

The principal seemed to consider that for a moment. "I'll take you to his classroom." The detectives followed Hardy down a couple of hallways. Hardy knocked on the door of one of the classrooms, opened it a foot, and stuck his head inside. "Mr. Aiken. You're needed outside, please." George Aiken came into the hall and closed the classroom door behind him. Aiken was six foot four inches tall, well built, and handsome. He had thick mink brown hair and hazel eyes. "What's wrong? Has something happened?" Aiken asked, looking back and forth between the detectives.

"Thank you, Mr. Hardy," Powers said. "We can take it from here." When the principal walked away, Powers and Dani performed the introduction routine.

"Do you happen to know where your wife is?" Dani asked.

Aiken shook his head. "Josie should be at work."

Dani asked, "When was the last time you saw her?"

"This morning. We got ready for work and left the house, as usual. I always leave at seven, and she leaves at seven thirty. Why? Why are you asking me this?"

"So, you drive separately to work?" Powers asked.

"Yes." Aiken looked back and forth between Dani and Powers. "What's going on? Is Josie alright?"

"Is there somewhere private we can go to talk?" Dani asked.

Aiken rubbed the back of his neck and nodded. "We can go to my office. Give me a moment, please." Aiken went back into the classroom, closing the door behind him.

Dani could hear him giving his students an assignment to work on in his absence.

Aiken came back into the hallway, but left the classroom door open. "This way," he said, motioning with his head.

Dani and Powers followed Aiken down the wide corridor to his office. It was small and neat. College diplomas hung on the wall. A framed photograph of George and Josie Aiken in formal attire sat on the desk. They looked happily married with their arms around each other, smiling.

Aiken sat at a small round conference table. "Please have a seat." Dani and Powers sat flanking Aiken. He looked back and forth between the two detectives again.

Powers explained that they had received a message threatening Josie. "She didn't go to work today. We went to your house but didn't find her there either. Is there somewhere else that she might have gone?"

Aiken shook his head. "No. No. She would have told me."

Dani and Powers looked at each other. Powers nodded. Dani removed the photograph of Josie and Cooke from her handbag and laid it on the table in front of Aiken.

Aiken picked up the picture, stared at it for a full minute, then set it back down. When he looked up, tears glistened in his eyes. "Jesus. That's Dayton. We all went to dinner together Saturday night."

"Did you know your wife was having an affair with Mr. Cooke?" Powers asked.

"Of course not." Aiken scrubbed his face with his hand. "How could she? Why? Why would she do this?"

"Right now we're concerned with finding your wife," Powers said. "What kind of car does she drive?"

"A Lexus sedan."

"Registered to her?" Powers asked.

"Yes."

Dani said, "Excuse me a moment." She stood and went out into the hallway, closing the office door behind her. Dani called dispatch on her cell phone. "We need an APB on a Lexus sedan registered to Josie Aiken." Next, she called Connie and explained who the woman in the photographs was and that she was missing. Dani gave her Josie's cell number, then said, "Contact the service provider and have them trace the phone."

Dani heard a loud crash inside the classroom. She ended the call with Connie and rushed back into Aiken's office. Dani saw that Aiken had hurled the photograph of himself and his wife against the wall, shattering the glass. Powers was standing beside the chair that he'd previously been sitting on, hand on his gun.

Dani walked over to stand in front of Aiken. He was staring with glazed eyes at the far wall, apparently seeing something else. Dani said, "Mr. Aiken. Is there anywhere else that you can think of that your wife might have gone?"

"I think you should ask Dayton Cooke that." Anger had taken over where sadness had been a few minutes earlier. "Obviously, he knew my wife better than I did."

Dani said, "We need a list of your wife's friends and family and their phone numbers. From you."

Aiken took a pad of paper and pen off of his office desk and sat back at the conference table. He removed his cell phone from his back pocket and tapped the contacts icon. Aiken transferred names and numbers from his phone to the paper. After he had finished, he ripped the sheet off of the pad and handed it to Dani. He stood and said, " Now, if you'll excuse me, I have a class to teach." With that, Aiken walked over to the door to his office, opened it, and waited for Dani and Powers to leave.

Dani handed Aiken a card as she exited the room. "Please check your home to see whether anything's out of place or missing. Josie's clothes, for example. Jewelry. Makeup. Give me a call if you find anything missing or think of anything else that might help us find your wife."

Aiken locked the door after them and walked away without saying another word. The sound of his heavy footsteps echoed in the empty hallway.

Dani shook her head. "Poor guy. The pain he must be feeling."

As they were walking back to the SUV, Powers asked, "You think Aiken honestly didn't know about the affair? Maybe he found out and did something to his wife."

"Unless he's an Academy Award actor, I don't think he knew before we showed him that photo."

From the SUV's mobile radio system, Dani and Powers heard the APB go out for Josie's car. The detectives drove to the bus station, looking for Josie's car in the parking lot. Not finding it there, they went to the airport and checked the lots. Powers drove slowly up and down each row. Josie's car wasn't there either.

When Dani's cell rang, she looked at the screen and said, "It's Connie." She listened, then said, "Got it. Thanks again for your help." Dani disconnected. "Josie's cell service provider said her phone's dead, so they can't track it. They'll contact us if it's turned back on."

Powers said. "We've done everything we can here. Let's head back to the office."

The detectives rode back to the Justice Center in silence, both lost in their own thoughts. As the two were making their way across the lobby, Dani suddenly stopped. She said, "We need to look at the camera footage of this building. Maybe we can see who left that manila envelope on Connie's desk."

"Good idea. I'll get Connie to set it up with IT."

When they reached the door to their office, Powers continued on to Connie's desk. Dani waved at her and walked inside. She stood in front of the copies of the photographs and note taped to the easel. "Where are you, Josie?" she whispered. Dani wrote the names of the people in the pictures below each one. She also made a notation of the affair and Josie's husband's name. Under the second message, Dani wrote the bible verses they had been taken from.

Powers came back into the office rubbing his hair. He sat at his desk and picked up the handset of his phone. "I'll check with the jail to see if Josie happens to be there."

Dani nodded. "I'll call the hospital." She checked the number from the listing of emergency contacts attached to her desk phone. Dani called the front desk and asked if they had a patient by the name of Josie Aiken. When the woman said Josie wasn't listed, Dani asked, "Have any unidentified women come in?" Powers was watching her. Dani shook her head and hung up the phone.

Powers said, "She's not at the jail either."

"Friends and family next," Dani said. She made a copy of the list that Aiken had provided. Dani counted the contacts. She drew a line under one of the names and handed the paper to Powers. "I'll take the first eleven, you take the last ten."

The two detectives got back on their phones and started calling. Dani found the process gut wrenching because she couldn't answer why they were looking for Josie. She also couldn't tell worried friends and relatives that Josie was safe. It didn't take long for Dani and Powers to finish their calls. Neither of them had gained any insight into where Josie might be. That left one appalling likelihood. Michael had her.

Dani and Powers were discussing next steps when a young man wearing jeans and a black t-shirt with a purple oxford over it entered the detectives' office. "I'm Emmerson Wilson from IT. I have the video footage from this morning ready for you to look at." Wilson had limp light brown hair in need of a cut, pale brown eyes, and a beak nose.

The detectives introduced themselves and shook Wilson's hand.

Wilson said, "Please follow me. We'll go to my office."

Dani and Powers followed Wilson upstairs. The IT Department was located in the south corner of the second floor. Wilson pulled three chairs in front of a desk. He sat in the middle chair. "Have a seat."

The detectives sat and watched the computer screen as Wilson tapped the keys on the keyboard. The main entrance and hallway came into view. The date and time were displayed in the lower left corner.

"We have one camera downstairs, one on the second floor, and one in each courtroom. What are you looking for?" Wilson asked, pushing his glasses up higher on the bridge of his nose.

"No idea," Dani said. "Anyone not in uniform or who doesn't look like they belong."

"All the side doors are kept locked," Powers said, thinking out loud. "The front doors are on a timer and automatically lock at six in the evening and unlock at seven. Unless you have a key card, you can't get in the building before seven. Connie got in at eight this morning. So, let's take a look at the video from seven to eight and see who shows up."

"Okay," Wilson said. He hit a few keys, and the video started playing at seven that morning. Nobody was around. Wilson fast forwarded to seven thirty. Two uniformed patrol deputies came in the side door.

"That's Willie Baines and Dan Foss," Powers said. "Probably just got off their shift."

The next person that showed up in the video entered the building at seven-fifty. That person was wearing jeans and a navy blue sweatshirt. The sweatshirt was zipped all the way up, and the hood was pulled over a plain dark blue baseball cap.

"Stop there," Dani said, leaning forward in her chair. "Who's that?"

Wilson tapped a key, and the video stopped.

"Definitely a man," Dani said. "Too tall and broad shouldered to be a woman. What do you think, Powers? Six two? A hundred ninety pounds?"

Powers nodded. "I'd say that's about right."

"Okay, go forward at regular speed," Dani said to Wilson.

As the video played, the man kept his head down and turned away.

Wilson said, "He knows where the camera is. He's avoiding it."

"Yep," Powers said. "You're definitely right about that."

The man stopped in front of Connie's desk. He removed a manila envelope from inside his sweatshirt and set it on the counter.

"Stop," Dani said. "Can you zoom in on his hands?"

"Sure." Wilson tapped keys until the man's hands took up most of the computer screen.

"Latex gloves," Dani said. "We're not going to find any fingerprints." Dani leaned even closer to the screen. "No rings, no tattoos, no identifying marks on his hands." Dani nodded at Wilson. "Okay, go forward." Dani quietly said, "Come on. Show us your face."

Head down, the man turned around and calmly walked back to the front door.

"Can't even see what color his hair is," Powers said.

At the front doors, the man stopped and unzipped his sweatshirt.

"What's he doing?" Powers asked.

With his back still to the camera, the man pulled a piece of paper out of the front of his sweatshirt and held it up. He turned it so that the camera could get a good shot of it.

Wilson tapped keys, and the video zoomed in. He whispered, "Oh, man. That can't be good."

Dani stared at the note on the screen. 'Dearest Dani. We'll talk soon. Love, Michael' was printed on the piece of paper in large letters. Dani's heart began racing, and her breathing became shallower. She stood and rushed out of the room. Dani flew down the stairs and out the front door. She ran around the corner of the building and leaned her back against the wall. Dani closed her eyes and tried to fight the panic that was filling her chest.

Suddenly, Tate Howland was standing beside Dani. "Take slow, deep breaths."

Dani's eyes flew open. "Get away from me."

"My sister gets panic attacks," Howland said. "It'll pass. Breathe deeply."

"Why can't you leave me be?"

"I'm not going to, no matter how much you push me away. So, you might as well stop."

"You're a pain, Tate. You know that?"

Tate smiled. "Back at ya', Dani."

Dani choked out a small laugh. She realized that the panic had abated somewhat and she could breathe better.

Howland leaned a shoulder against the wall next to Dani. "Have you had panic attacks before?"

"Yes. But, not in years." Dani hesitated. "If people find out it could hurt my career."

"Hey, your secret's safe with me."

Dani pushed off from the wall. "I better get back." As she made her way upstairs, Dani took deep breaths, trying to slow her racing heart.

When Dani walked back into Wilson's office, Powers asked, "What the hell was that?"

"I needed some air."

Powers frowned. "I had Emmerson print a screenshot of the guy holding up the piece of paper, as well as a close-up of the typed note."

Dani sat back down. "Can you pull up the video from yesterday afternoon? About two?"

"Sure, "Wilson said. "No problem."

Dani looked at Powers. "Maybe we can get a shot of the boy that delivered the first note to Connie. If we can find the kid, he might be able to give us a description of Michael."

"Good call," Powers said.

Wilson finished tapping on his computer keyboard, and the video started playing. They watched until they saw a boy in blue jeans and a red sweatshirt come in the front door. He had a manila envelope in his hand.

"That's him," Dani said. "Can you get a close-up shot of his face and print it?"

Wilson tapped on the keys. "Done." A piece of paper spit out of the printer next to his desk.

"Thanks, Emmerson," Dani said. "We appreciate the help."

"Anytime." Wilson handed Dani the print outs of Michael and the boy.

Powers squinted at Wilson. "It goes without saying that you can't mention this to anyone."

"Of... of course," Wilson stammered. "No problem."

The two detectives went downstairs to Tirrell's office and showed him the screenshots.

Powers said, "This guy's slick. He'd been to the Center before. He'd scoped out where the cameras were and what time Connie gets to work."

Tirrell said, "Patrol's still looking for the Aiken woman's car. No sign of it." He rubbed a stubby finger across the end of his nose and yawned. "It's late. I want you two to go home. Get some dinner. Rest. There's not a dang thing more you can do tonight."

Dani said. "We should look through past videos and see if we can find a man checking out the cameras."

Tirrell said, "Not tonight."

"Sir, I'd like to..." Dani didn't get to finish what she was saying.

Tirrell interrupted. "That's an order, McKenna."

Powers and Dani stood to leave.

"McKenna. Be extra alert," Tirrell said. "Just as a precaution. I don't like that he's fixated on you."

"Yes, sir. Will do. Thank you, sir."

Dani was rushing across the lobby when Tate Howland came down the stairs.

"Dani," Howland said. "Hold up a sec."

"I can't. I have to get home."

Tate jogged after Dani. He caught up with her at the front doors. Dani was swiping her key card through the card access reader to unlock the door.

Tate followed Dani outside. "Hey. Powers told me about the note you got yesterday. And, Tirrell mentioned the one you got this morning. Any luck finding out who the woman is?"

"We've identified her, but she's missing." Dani continued to walk to her Jeep. "We have an APB out." Dani clicked the remote to unlock the door.

Tate rushed ahead and opened the door for her.

"Thanks." Dani flung her handbag on the passenger seat and started the Jeep. When she reached to close the door, Tate held onto it, forcing Dani to look up at him.

Tate pulled a business card and pen out of the inside pocket of his suit jacket. He scribbled on the card and handed it to Dani. "I know you can take care of yourself. But, this is my cell number. In case you decide you want someone safe to talk to."

Dani glanced at the card, then up into Tate's chocolate brown eyes. "Thanks." She pulled the door shut, started the engine and drove away.

Tate stood in the parking lot and watched Dani until he could no longer see her Jeep.

When Dani got home, she took Bo out for a short walk, then fed him. "Sorry I'm so late, boy." As Bo ate, Dani made herself a turkey and avocado sandwich. She changed into sweats, started a fire, and curled up in the armchair in front of it. She'd only finished half of the sandwich when her cell phone rang. Dani looked at the screen, but the number was unavailable. She swiped the answer icon and said, "Detective McKenna."

A disembodied voice said, "Hello Dani. I see you're awake very late this evening."

Dani jumped up, spun around, and looked out the large front windows. Bo sprang to his feet and started growling. Dani held up her hand, and Bo quieted. "Who is this?"

"It's Michael… I hope I'm not the reason that you're still up."

53

Dani turned the living room lights off and walked over to the front windows. She looked outside but didn't see anyone. "What do you want?"

"I wanted to talk to you."

Dani walked through the house, looking out of each window. "About what?"

"About Josie, of course."

Dani stopped mid-stride. "Where is she?"

"Well, Dani. You see. That's part of the fun. I take them, and you try to find them before it's too late."

Dani went into her bedroom and took her Glock out of the holster. Holding it at her side, she said, "That's not fun. That's sick."

"No, Dani. It's not sick." Even though he was using a voice changer, Michael's tone went from sweet to angry. "I'm following the word of the Lord." His tone changed back to friendly again. "I look forward to talking to you again soon, Dani. I love you."

"Wait! Tell me where Josie is." Dani realized that she wasn't talking to anyone. Michael had already disconnected the call. Bo leaned against Dani and looked up at her.

Dani rushed through the living room, grabbing her glass of wine off of the coffee table as she went by. She hurried into the master bathroom and set her Glock on the counter. Opening the top drawer, Dani rifled through the contents. She finally found the prescription bottle marked 'Xanax'. Dani opened the top and poured two pills into the palm of her shaking hand. She tossed the two pills into her mouth and washed them down with the wine. Dani took her Glock and wine glass back to the kitchen. Refilling the glass, Dani drank the contents without taking a breath. Then she started checking the locks on all the doors and windows.

CHAPTER 3

When Dani's cell phone rang at three thirty in the morning, she was still awake. She sat straight up in bed and looked at the bedside clock. It had only been four hours since Dani had phoned Powers, relaying the call from Michael. Powers had asked if she wanted him to come over. She had declined. Dani checked the caller identification on the phone and saw that the call was from dispatch. "Detective McKenna."

"Dani. It's Wallis. Patrol found the Aiken woman's car."

"Fantastic." Dani opened the top drawer of her bedside table and pulled out a notepad and pen. "Give me the address."

"Corner of Second Street and Seventh Avenue West. Salvation Church."

Dani mumbled, "You're kidding me?"

"Sorry. Didn't catch that."

"Nothing. Who else has been notified?"

"I called Powers first. He said to call you next and tell you to meet him there. Then he asked me to call Nash, Paget, and Alyce.

But, Nash is the one who found the car, so he's already there. Securing the scene."

"Thanks, Wallis. I'm on my way."

Dani dressed as quickly as possible and rushed out of the house. When she arrived less than fifteen minutes after dispatch had phoned, she wasn't surprised to see Powers already on site. He lived in town, so he was closer.

The sheriff's office had a highly trained crime scene team that included five detectives, eight patrol deputies, and one evidence technician. Dani and Powers were both on the team. The three additional detectives worked on a rotational, part-time basis.

Todd Nash was one of the patrol deputies on the team. Nash was average height, extremely buff, and shaved both his face and head. He smiled at Dani when she walked over to where he and Powers were standing. Nash said, "Hey. How are you doing? Powers has been filling me in on your crazy Bible guy."

Dani gave Nash a small smile. "Glad you found the car."

Powers patted Nash on the shoulder. "Thanks for securing the scene. Go ahead and take off. You've been on duty all night. We can take it from here."

Nash nodded. "See you at the Center."

When Nash had driven away, Powers walked over to his vehicle. He came back and handed Dani a lidded white paper cup. "Coffee. Cream and sugar. I knew you wouldn't take time to make any."

"Thanks," Dani said, taking the mug. "I sure can use it."

Norton Paget drove up. He parked in front of the crime scene tape that had been strung between trees on either side of Seventh Avenue. Paget was one of the rotational detectives on the crime scene team. Alyce Ryder, the department's evidence technician, was sitting in the passenger seat. They both got out of the car and walked over to Dani and Powers.

As the lead detective, Powers assumed command. "Everyone listen up." The team gathered around Powers in the middle of the street. He explained about the notes Dani had received and the missing woman. "I'll prepare the narrative and diagrams, and handle initial photos. When I'm done, I'll vacuum and help Ryder with swabbing. Ryder, you'll collect latents inside the car. McKenna, you're in charge of the outside of the car. Paget, you've got evidence around the car. You all know what to do. Let's get it done."

Each team member had been issued a complete crime scene kit so that any one of them could perform a required duty. Each member kept their kit bag in their work vehicle. Powers and Dani had driven their private cars, so they took the equipment they would need out of Ryder's kit. Outside of the cordoned off area, they each donned protective coveralls with a hood. They also put on gloves and booties. Paget set up several lights to illuminate the entire area around the car.

Powers started by taking photographs of the exterior of the car. He photographed each side, each corner, the front, and the rear. Powers also took a shot of the tag and the VIN. Next, he photographed the interior of the vehicle.

Each of the four team members took a section of the inside of the car and started to search. They each bagged what they found and entered it on an evidence log sheet. Powers vacuumed the soft surfaces with the team's microparticle collection vacuum. When Powers finished, he looked at Dani and said, "No sign of blood anywhere."

Dani began processing the outside of the car for latent fingerprints and palm prints. Ryder handled the inside. Powers swabbed the steering wheel and seat belts for DNA. Paget placed an evidence marking stand on the ground next to items that he found in the street and on the sidewalk. He took photographs of each item.

During this six hour process, the sun came up over the horizon and rose in the sky. A few people emerged from their houses and watched for a while. Most became quickly bored with the tedium and went back inside.

After the team members had finished their tasks, Ryder collected their booties. They would be sent for processing, in case they had any evidence on them. Each team member also placed their protective clothing in a separate bag. Ryder documented each piece. These would be saved until Powers was confident they wouldn't be needed. Ryder gathered the evidence bags and logs from each team member. She loaded them into an evidence box in the back of Paget's SUV. Ryder said, "I'll get all the evidence and latents over to the state crime lab first thing."

"Thanks for all your help," Powers said to Ryder. He shook hands with Paget and thanked him also.

"See you back at the Center," Paget said as he got into his vehicle.

Dani called dispatch. "Please arrange for a tow truck to pick up Josie Aiken's car and take it to impound." She disconnected, then called Connie. "Last night I wrote the justification for a warrant for Josie Aiken's phones. But, the judges had already left for the evening. Would you get it off of my desk and take it upstairs?"

"Of course," Connie said.

"Thanks. Appreciate the help." Dani tapped the red end call icon on her cell phone.

"I'm starving," Powers said. "Hop in my truck. Let's go eat. We'll come back and interview neighbors after that."

"Sounds good." Dani grabbed her handbag out of her Jeep, locked it, and got into Powers' truck.

They had only gone two blocks when Powers' cell phone rang. "It's Connie," he told Dani, looking at the caller identification on the screen. He swiped the answer icon. "What's up?" Powers listened for a few seconds, then said, "Text me those coordinates. Dani's with me. We'll head straight there. Have dispatch contact Ryder, Paget, Nash, and Mercer. Have them meet us there. And, get whichever patrol deputy is closest to secure the area." He listened for a moment, then ended the call.

"What's happening?" Dani asked.

"Josie's cell provider called. Her phone's back on."

Powers and Dani sped west on U.S. Highway 2. The GPS said to turn right on Marquardt Lane, then right again onto North Hill Road.

Dani quoted from the first note that she'd received. "In your hills shall they fall that are slain with the sword. Hill Road."

Powers glanced at Dani. "I hope you're wrong."

When the two arrived, they saw that Kevin Mercer was already there. Mercer had parked his patrol car south of the coordinates. Powers pulled into the middle of the road next to Mercer's vehicle.

Mercer was one of the eight patrol deputies on the crime scene team. He was tall and thin. He was bald on top and kept the sides of his dark hair cut very short. Mercer walked over and greeted Powers and Dani. Then he asked, "What's going on?"

Powers filled Mercer in, then said, "Glad you were the closest patrol unit."

The area to the east of North Hill Road was heavily wooded with Ponderosa Pine trees that grew all the way to the edge of the blacktop. West of the road there was flat row crop land. Searching for a five inch cell phone was going to take time.

"Let's get the road secured," Powers said. "I'll block off the south end, after the driveway into that house over there." Powers pointed. "Mercer, you block it off on that north curve, before the intersection."

Mercer nodded. He got into his vehicle and drove along the edge of the road to the place that Powers had indicated. Mercer parked across the street, completely blocking it. Powers drove south and did the same with his SUV.

Norton Paget arrived. He parked next to Mercer's car. Alyce Ryder was again in his vehicle. They both got out and walked over to Powers. Paget said, "Hadn't even made it back to the Center when we got the call."

Within seconds, Todd Nash arrived in his patrol vehicle and parked next to Paget's SUV. Everyone greeted the others and gathered around Powers.

Powers looked around. "Like the proverbial needle in a haystack. Mercer, Dani and I will take the woods. Nash, Paget, Ryder, you take the crop area. Walk the area in grids. If anyone spots anything, call on the radio."

Dani, Powers, and Mercer spaced themselves an arm's length away from each other. They started searching on the north end of the forested area. There wasn't much undergrowth but once bright green pine needles littered the ground. The three moved in an easterly direction.

They had been working their third swath for several minutes when Dani's scalp prickled. She stopped dead still in her tracks. Dani closed her eyes and listened for what had alerted her subconscious. She heard a faint buzzing coming from her right.

Powers saw Dani stop. He spoke into his radio. "McKenna. What have you got?"

Dani unclipped the radio from her belt and said, "Not sure." She walked toward the sound. Six paces ahead she found the source of the noise. Dani took several shallow breaths, then pressed the transmit button on her radio. Her voice was shaky as she said, "It's Josie. She's dead."

Josie Aiken was naked. She'd been posed, sitting with her back against the orange-red trunk of a pine tree. Josie's elbows were tied behind her with nylon cable ties. This forced her back to arch and her breasts to protrude. Josie's legs were spread wide on the ground. Flies swarmed the numerous stab wounds on her chest and groin. Blood had run down her torso. Josie's head lolled to one side. Her eyes were wide open, staring vacantly forward. Josie's cell phone had been placed on the ground between her legs.

Powers came up behind Dani. He feverishly ran his hand back and forth over his hair. "What kind of person does that to another human being?"

When Mercer saw the body, he covered his mouth and started gagging. He turned and sprinted a few yards away. Mercer bent over at the waist, placing his hands on his knees and retched.

Dani felt like her lungs were being squeezed by an invisible force. She tried to take a deep breath, but only managed to inhale a meager amount of faintly rust smelling air. A tear slid down her cheek.

Powers squatted next to the body. "Not much blood. She was killed somewhere else." He stood back up and keyed the microphone on his radio. He called the other searchers, telling them to bring a body bag and their crime scene kits over.

~~~

Eleven hours later, Dani and Powers sat in the chairs in front of Corporal Tirrell's desk and briefed him. Powers said, "The area around the body was clean. We didn't find any evidence."

Tirrell nodded. "While you were out today, Judge Bartel signed the warrant for Aiken's cell phone. The service provider is going to fax Connie the call logs as soon as they have them."

Powers said, "At least that's good news."

Tirrell said, "Also, we got the results of the crime lab's analysis on the envelopes, notes, and photographs. No latents on any of them. And, he used tap water to moisten the glue on the envelopes."

Powers leaned his elbows on his knees. "So, this guy's smart. Hopefully, there will be some evidence on Josie's body. Maybe she put up a fight, and the lab will find his DNA under her fingernails."

Tirrell said, "I called Les Michaels earlier." When neither of the detectives showed any recognition of the name, Tirrell said. "Michaels is the SAIC at the FBI's Salt Lake City field office. He's sending their office's behavioral profiling expert to help us get a handle on the perp. I had Connie send him copies of the notes from Michael so he could be looking at them on the plane ride over." Tirrell looked up at the clock hanging on his wall above the door. He rubbed his eye with a finger. "It's almost midnight. Go home.

Get some food and rest. Be back here early tomorrow. We need to find this guy."

"Yes, sir," Dani said, pushing herself out of the chair with her arms.

Powers nodded, stood, and followed Dani out of the room. His footsteps were heavy as he trod down the hallway. In the office, Powers flopped down onto his desk chair with a loud sigh. He pulled the top drawer open and removed a bottle of Jameson whiskey.

Dani sat on her chair, powered up her computer, and opened the email from the crime lab. She read the test results for the items they had received from Michael. Dani wanted to be sure that there wasn't something the sheriff had missed. He hadn't.

Dani said, "I'll get the Murder Book started." She took a large three-ring binder out of her desk drawer. She inserted a table of contents sheet and dividers. Dani set up separate tabs for the notes from Michael, the photographs of Josie that he had sent, transcripts of his phone calls, forensic reports, and crime scene photos.

Powers took two paper cups out of the drawer and poured some whiskey in each. He placed one of the cups on Dani's desk and held up his. "Today was rough."

Dani leaned over her desk and took the cup. She tapped it against Powers' and sipped. Dani choked, blowing out through her mouth. She coughed. "I don't drink hard liquor."

Powers leaned back in his chair and put both feet on the top of his desk. "Never?"

Dani shook her head.

"What do you drink? Wait... you do drink, don't you?"

Dani chuckled. "Yes. But, only wine." She read the lab's report out loud.

Powers sipped from his cup and studied Dani's face as she read.

When she'd finished reading, Dani looked over at Powers and saw him staring at her. "What?" She rubbed her hands over her face, checking for something that might be on it.

"I was wondering why a woman as good looking as you doesn't have a boyfriend? Or, even go out on dates? Guys must hit on you all the time, but as far as I can tell, the only male in your life is Bo."

A shadow crossed Dani's eyes. She drank, feeling the burn of the whiskey as it slid down her throat. Dani shrugged.

"We've worked together for almost two years, and I still know next to nothing about you," Powers said. Holding out the bottle of whiskey, he reached across his desk and poured a little more into

Dani's cup. Powers added some to his own cup, then relaxed back again. "You've told me that your dad died when you were young. Your mom remarried five years later. And, you have a stepbrother. That's it."

Dani silently stared at the golden liquid inside her cup.

"I was married for eight months. A long time ago. My girlfriend got pregnant, so I did the right thing. But, I didn't want to be tied down. I was a crap husband. She miscarried, and I bailed." After a minute of silence, Powers threw up his hands. "See. This is how being partners and friends are supposed to work, McKenna. I tell you something personal, and you reciprocate." He paused, frowning. "Did you have a bad breakup or something? Is that why you don't date?"

Dani sat in silence for a few more seconds. Then she said, "I don't trust people. I live with a dog because I trust him completely."

Powers intense eyes softened. "Well, I hope you know you can trust me, Dani. I've got your back. Always."

Feeling extremely uncomfortable, Dani mumbled, "Thanks." She hoped sharing time was over.

"Everyone needs to have at least one human being that they trust in their life, McKenna. Nobody's an island." Powers swallowed the rest of the Jamison in his cup and threw it in the wastebasket. He stood. "I'm headed home. See you tomorrow." Powers walked toward the door, then stopped and turned back to Dani. "I hope like hell that bringing in the FBI doesn't turn this investigation into a cluster."

Dani nodded. "Me too." She finished the remaining whiskey in her cup and threw it away. Dani took her handbag out of the bottom drawer and headed to the hall. Out of the corner of her eye, she noticed that a fax was sitting in the machine behind Connie's desk. Dani walked over and removed the papers. It was the call log from Josie's cell service provider.

Dani went back to her desk to look over the list of calls. She skimmed the names, skipping over the women. Dani made a copy and began checking off names and their corresponding numbers from the list of friends and family that George Aiken had provided. There were seventeen unidentified numbers left. Suddenly, Dani thought of the time and looked at the clock on the wall. Out loud, she said, "Bo." She left the original fax on Powers' desk and stuck the copy into her handbag. She grabbed her jacket off the back of the chair and hurried down the hallway.

Dani drove home on autopilot, her attention turned inward to Josie's death and the past. She fed Bo first thing when she got inside the house. "I'm going to buy an automatic feeder right now, boy. I don't want you having to go hungry again if I can't get home." Dani's feet felt like lead weights as she climbed the spiral staircase to the left of the living room. The stairs led to a guest bedroom and bath on one side of the hall and a home office on the other. Dani sat down heavily on her desk chair. She placed both of her hands on her back and arched backward, stretching. Dani pulled up several websites and looked at different dog feeders. She quickly chose one and paid extra for next day delivery.

Dani went back downstairs to the kitchen and poured herself a glass of Chardonnay. She took the foil covered half sandwich from the previous night out of the refrigerator. Dani set the wine, food, and call log from Josie Aiken's cell phone on the island. She ate as she read the log. Dani finished the sandwich. Sipping wine, she stared at the pages. Then, Dani said, "Come on boy. Let's go for a ride."

Dani drove to the Aiken's home. Bo happily wagged his tail the entire ride. He stuck his head out the passenger window, ears flapping in the wind. Dani left Bo in the Jeep with the window down and walked around to the front of the house. Dani could see George Aiken sitting in the living room on the couch. He was holding his head in his hands, and staring into a tumbler of amber colored liquor that sat on the coffee table. She knocked on the front door.

When Aiken looked over and saw Dani, he got up and slowly walked to the door. Aiken opened the front door but didn't say anything.

Dani's heart ached for the man. He looked like he'd aged ten years in one day. Lines that hadn't been noticeable yesterday were etched into his face. She asked, "May I come in?"

Aiken stood to one side to allow Dani to enter. He moved back to the couch and sat again. "Want a drink?"

"No. Thank you." Dani sat in a mid-century yellow armchair across from Aiken. "I'm so sorry for your loss."

Aiken picked up the glass and gulped a mouthful of liquor. "What can I do for you, detective?"

"I wanted to know if you'd checked Josie's things to see if anything's missing."

Aiken nodded woodenly and stared out the front wall of glass. "Everything's like she left it... except now it's all different."

Dani took Josie's cell phone log out of her handbag and set it on the coffee table. "This is a log of Josie's calls for the past month. Would you look this over and see if there are any calls from someone you don't know."

In a monotone voice, Aiken asked, "Why?"

"There might be something that could help us find the person that murdered your wife."

71

Aiken drained the tumbler. The clinking sound of glass meeting glass filled the room as he set it on the tabletop. He picked up the log and began reading.

Dani handed him a black pen from her handbag. "If you'd mark the names you don't recognize, that would really help." Dani sat quietly as Aiken went through each page.

After ten minutes, Aiken handed it back. He picked up the tumbler, saw that it was empty, and set it back down. "Sure are a lot of calls to and from Dayton on there."

Dani stood. "Thank you, Mr. Aiken. I appreciate your help. I'll show myself out now." She moved toward the front door, then turned around. "Again, I'm so sorry for your loss." Dani knew that the man was grieving not only for the death of his wife, but for her betrayal. As Dani closed the door behind herself, she saw Aiken go to the kitchen and refill his glass.

Dani was glad to have Bo with her, but as she drove she realized that her sadness had transferred to him. Bo sat on the passenger seat but didn't put his head out the window. Instead, he watched Dani. She rubbed his ears on the way back home. Dani couldn't shake Aiken's tortured face from her mind.

In the kitchen, Dani picked up the now warm glass of wine and stuck it in the refrigerator. She took the wine bottle out and poured another glass. Dani carried it to the living room where she sat on the couch, tucking her feet under her. Bo sat next to her on the bright multi-colored area rug. Dani stroked her hand down Bo's back as she sipped wine. She looked out the window at the lake shining in the moonlight and thought about the acute bitter pain of loss.

Dani had almost finished the glass of wine when her cell rang. She pulled the phone out of its holster and looked at the caller identification. Seeing 'unavailable' on the screen, Dani quickly set the wine glass on the coffee table. She rushed into her bedroom with Bo following after her. As the phone continued to ring, Dani pulled a small voice recorder out of the top drawer of her nightstand. She set the phone and the recorder on it next to each other. Dani sat on the side of her bed and hit the record button. She swiped the answer icon on the cell phone screen and put the phone on speaker. "Detective McKenna."

"Dani. You're up late again tonight."

"What do you want, Michael?"

"Don't be rude. I wanted to talk to you. I assume you found Josie."

"You turned her phone on. You wanted us to find her."

"Not us. I only care about you. Not the others. They don't matter. Only you."

Dani closed her eyes and sucked in an unsteady breath. "Why? Why me?"

"Because you're perfect. From the moment I first saw you, I knew you were the only woman for me. You're pure and innocent. Unlike Josie. She was a poor substitute for you. She might have looked as beautiful as you, but she was the opposite. That's why she had to die."

"You don't know anything about me. I'm not pure and innocent."

"Yes, you are. Because I'm the only man for you."

"I don't know who you are."

"Of course you do." He paused. "We'll talk more about it when I call tomorrow night. Sleep well, Dani. I love you."

Dani took the bottle of Xanax out of the drawer in the nightstand next to her bed. She carried it back to the living room. Shaking two white pills into her hand, she swallowed them with the rest of the wine in her glass. Dani refilled it, drinking as she moved from one end of the house to the other. In each room, she tried to open the windows, assuring that all the locks were still engaged. Dani wiggled the knob on each door back and forth checking that they wouldn't turn.

After Dani had finished, she sat back down on the couch and drank some wine. The muffled tapping of the heel of her boot hitting the rug was the only sound in the room. Dani gulped down the rest of the wine in her glass. Then, she stood back up and started through the house again, confirming that each lock was secured and the security system was armed.

CHAPTER 4

Dani hadn't been able to fall asleep for several hours after the phone call from Michael. The last time she'd checked the digital clock on her nightstand, it was four-eleven in the morning.

When Bo woke Dani up by licking her face, she was relieved. She'd been having a horrible nightmare where she was being tortured by Michael. Dani rubbed the top of Bo's head. "I'm okay, boy." She looked at the clock and saw that it was five thirty in the morning. Dani got out of bed, showered, and dressed for work. In the living room, she picked up the bottle of Xanax, opened it, and shoved four pills into the front pocket of her pants.

Dani drove to the nearest convenience store to buy coffee. She filled two tall to-go cups with coffee and added plenty of cream and sugar. Walking out of the store she saw that clouds had darkened the sky. As Dani drove, a thin rain, white as cut glass, started to fall. Traffic passed as a smooth hiss on the wet road. As Dani made her way to the Center, she drank one of the cups of coffee. She took the second cup to her office.

Dani sat at her desk and began typing on her computer's keyboard. She searched for synonyms of the word sorceress. After reading the results, she said out loud, "That's got to be it." Dani stood and began writing on the easel standing next to her desk. She wrote 'an enchantress breaks men's hearts below Michael's note about not letting a sorceress live. Next, Dani looked up the bible verse of the second note. She wrote 'Exodus 22:18' on the easel. Dani stared at the photographs of Josie Aiken and whispered, "I'm sorry we didn't save you."

Powers walked into the room. "You get any sleep last night after your call from Michael?"

Dani shrugged. "A little. You?"

Powers shook his head. "Not much. Couldn't get the image of Josie's mutilated body out of my head."

"I've been doing some research." Dani pointed at the whiteboard. "Some synonyms of sorceress are enchantress and seductress. Someone who breaks men's hearts. I think one of the reasons Josie was chosen was because she was having an affair."

Powers sat at his desk and read the whiteboard. "That makes some sort of sick sense," he said, running his hand back and forth over his hair.

"The offender would also have found her sexually attractive."

Dani and Powers both looked toward the door and at the man who had spoken.

"FBI Assistant SAIC, Hal Verity," the short, thin man said as he stepped inside. Verity had wavy black hair that was held in place by some type of product. He had a strong chin and a nose that was slightly flattened. His eyebrows and mouth both turned down at the corners, giving the impression that he frowned perpetually.

Two men in white dress shirts and ties followed after Verity. Each was carrying a large black leather computer portfolio, which they set on top of the empty desks in the office. They began unloading their cases and hooking up laptops.

Dani recognized the two men from the local FBI office. The one on the right was Special Agent Archie Richards and on the left was Special Agent Peter Webb. Neither one said a word or made eye contact.

Powers stood. "What do you think you're doing?"

Tirrell marched into the room. "The feds are taking over the case."

Powers face flushed with anger. "What the hell?! Why?! This is our case!"

Verity answered. "Federal jurisdiction."

Powers looked at Tirrell. "The hell!"

Tirrell held up a thick hand. "Calm down. They're in the right. This case includes kidnapping, abusive sexual conduct, and torture. One would be sufficient, but all three fall under the jurisdiction of the feds. Les Michaels told me that you two are integral to this case and that you'll be part of the FBI's task force."

Powers laugh was brittle, like a glass breaking. "Well, that's just peachy of him."

Verity said, "You must be Detectives Cliff Powers and Danielle McKenna."

Dani said, "I prefer Dani."

Verity nodded.

Tirrell said, "Special Agent Verity's an expert on this type of murder." The sheriff looked first at Dani, then at Powers. "He's in charge. Everyone takes their lead from him. Are you clear on that?"

Powers sat back on his desk chair and growled, "Clear."

Dani said, "Yes, sir."

Satisfied, Tirrell turned and went back to his office.

Verity moved to the front of the room and said, "The first thing we need to do is establish roles. I will be the liaison to the

victim's family and the surrounding law enforcement agencies."
Detective Powers, you will be the liaison to the prosecutor's
office, the forensic laboratory, your crime scene team, and
supporting patrol officers."

Powers said, "So, you'll take over Corporal Tirrell's duties,
and I'll keep doing what I've always done. Sounds good."

Dani tried to break the tension. She looked at Verity. "You
said Michael would have found Josie sexually attractive. What
else can you tell us?"

Verity pulled the whiteboard to the front of the room and
tapped the photograph of Josie's mutilated body. "This type of
murder is referred to as a lust murder. Most cases of lust murder
involve male perpetrators. These offenders have made a
connection between murder and sexual gratification. The
offender stabs, cuts, pierces, and mutilates the sexual regions of
the victim's body. Lust murders also include activities such as
posing the body." Verity looked at the two detectives. "And,
there's always more than one victim."

Dani squeezed her eyes shut. The vision of Josie's bloody
body appeared in her mind.

Verity said, "Detective McKenna, I understand that the perp's
communicating with you."

Dani opened her eyes. "Yes. And, he called again last night." She pulled the recorder out of her handbag, set it on her desk, and pushed the play button. Everyone gathered around Dani and listened to the recording. When the conversation ended, she pushed the stop button.

Verity asked, "Any idea why he's contacting you?"

"No." Dani straightened the pen, marker, and pad of paper on the top of her desk.

Verity watched her, then asked, "You sure about that?"

Powers said, "Dani was headed upstairs to IT to get them to set up a trace on her phones. If that's okay with you, of course."

Dani silently thanked Powers for taking the spotlight off of her. On the way upstairs, she detoured into the women's restroom. Dani checked that the two stalls were empty before pulling a Xanax from the front pocket of her pants. She tossed the small pill into her mouth. A bitter taste assailed her tongue. Dani turned on the sink's water faucet and stuck her mouth under it, washing the Xanax down. She continued on to IT, finding Emmerson Wilson sitting at his desk.

"Hey, Dani. How's it going?"

"I need your help again, Emmerson."

"Sure. What do you need?"

Dani explained about the calls that she'd received, and the need to put a trace on her work and cell phones.

Wilson started typing on his computer keyboard. "Check that the numbers we have are correct."

Dani leaned in and looked at Wilson's computer monitor. "Those are correct."

"I'll set up the future traces first," Wilson said. "It'll take a little while to trace the two cell calls you've already received."

"So, how exactly do the traces work?" Wilson's face became animated. Dani doubted anyone had ever asked him about the technology.

"The phone company uses what's called Automatic Number Identification, or ANI, to capture the billing number of the calling party." Wilson's voice turned excited. "Of course, that doesn't work for prepaid cell phones. For those, we use what's called the Visitor/Home Location Registers. The registers identify which cell tower the call's originating from. And, the caller doesn't need to talk for two minutes like in the movies. The trace can begin before you even pick up."

"So, I should let the phone ring as long as possible."

"That wouldn't hurt." Wilson pushed his glasses up with his index finger.

"Got it. Thanks. I really appreciate your help."

Wilson smiled broadly. "Anytime."

Dani went back to her office. "Done." She looked at Verity, who was now sitting at a foldable table that had been moved into the room. "What else can you tell us about these lust murders?"

Verity stood and walked to the front of the room like he was a professor about to give a classroom lecture. "Lust murders are classified as organized or disorganized. Michael's an organized offender. He's probably above average in intelligence. He's methodical and cunning. His murders are carefully planned. He avoids leaving evidence behind and is aware of police procedures. The victim's bodies are often removed from the actual crime scene. The offender might do this to taunt the police or to prevent discovery by transporting the body to another location. He takes pride in his ability to thwart the police investigation. And, he's likely to follow news reports of the event." Verity paused and looked at Dani. "Any idea why this perp has chosen you?"

"No. No idea."

Verity said, "He's someone you know."

Powers shook his head. "Oh, come on. Isn't it just as likely that it's someone Dani's met at a random place? Like the supermarket bag boy. Or, the guy where she buys coffee."

Verity's brown creased as he glowered at Powers. "I believe it's someone she knows better than that. It's personal for him." Verity pulled another whiteboard to the front of the room. He picked up a dry erase marker. "We will have a daily briefing every morning at eight. Detective Powers, could you tell us on where you are in the investigation and what actions you were planning next?"

Powers leaned forward in his chair and started counting off on his fingers. "We need to interview the people who live on the street where Josie's car was left, as well as where her body was placed. We need to follow up on Josie's cell phone logs, in case Michael called her. And, we need to review past videos of the Center to see if we can see a guy checking out the location of the cameras." Powers explained about the videos Emmerson Wilson had played for them the day before.

Dani said, "As I was leaving last night, I found Josie's cell log in Connie's fax machine." She motioned with her head. "The original is on your desk. I went to the Aiken's house and had George look at it." Dani picked up her copy of the log and handed it to Powers. "He marked the numbers he didn't recognize. Some of them are probably work related. We should have Dayton Cooke look at the log."

Powers shot Dani a concerned look. "Until Michael's caught, I'd prefer it if you didn't go out at night by yourself. It's not safe."

"I wasn't alone. Bo was with me. Besides, I'm not going to hide. I have a job to do."

"Who's Bo?" Verity asked.

Dani said, "My dog."

"Very protective," Powers said.

Verity said, "Anyway... I will interview George Aiken to find out everything we can about his wife. Her habits, friends, hobbies. Also, what she did the week before the murder. Richards, I want you on past video of the Justice Center."

Richards had a face like the surface of the moon. The craters gave him the appearance of being tough as nails. In opposition, his voice was so high pitched that it almost squeaked. "You got it, boss."

Verity continued, "Webb, I want you to follow up with Mr. Cooke on Mrs. Aiken's cell phone log."

"I'm on it, boss." Webb was much older than the other two FBI agents. The top of his head was nearly bald, with unruly graying hair on the sides that gave him a mad scientist vibe.

After both agents had exited the office, Dani said, "We also need to find the kid that delivered the first note. He might be able to give us a description of Michael. I did an internet search, looking for schools within walking distance of the Justice Center. From the video, the boy looked too old to go to the nearby elementary school. The Catholic school only goes up to eighth grade. That leaves Flathead High School. I'd like to take the photo of the kid there and see if they can ID him."

Verity said, "Detective McKenna, since you're on top of that, I'd like you to search for him."

Powers rolled his eyes, then said, "I'll go interview the neighbors where the body was placed."

Even though Powers didn't ask for his permission, Verity nodded his concurrence. "I'll speak with people along the street where Mrs. Aiken's car was abandoned."

The three gathered what they needed and walked down the corridor together. Tate Howland came down the stairs and met them in the lobby. "I hear we have a body."

Powers introduced Verity and gave Howland a quick update. "We'll keep you informed."

"I appreciate that," Howland said. "Dani, be careful out there."

Dani looked at the linoleum floor in front of her feet. "Right." She headed for the front doors.

Powers patted Howland on the back. "See you soon."

Howland went back upstairs and watched Dani through the window of his office. Verity sat in his rental car in the parking lot and watched Howland watch Dani.

Dani drove to Flathead High, parked in front of the sidewalk leading to the entrance, and jogged inside. She introduced herself to the woman at the reception area in the office. Dani pulled the photograph of the boy out of her handbag and laid it on the smooth white countertop. "We're trying to identify this young man. We need to speak to him regarding an ongoing investigation. Can you tell me if you recognize him?"

The woman picked up reading glasses and put them on. She studied the photograph and shook her head. "Sorry. I don't."

"Is there someone else who might be able to identify him? Maybe the principal or vice-principal?"

"I'll get them for you." The woman turned on the intercom system that sat on the counter and called the principal and vice-principal to the office.

The principal arrived first. He introduced himself and looked at the boy's photograph. "I don't recognize him. Sorry."

The vice-principal arrived a short minute later. He studied the photograph. "I've met every person that attends school here. This young man does not." He handed the picture back to Dani.

Dani thanked them and walked back to her Jeep, thinking about where else the boy might go to school. Inside the Jeep, Dani opened the internet on her phone and looked at nearby schools. There was an alternative high school on First Avenue. Dani drove the few blocks to the Lindeman Education Center. Both parking spaces in front were occupied, so Dani parked in front of a yellow painted curb. She pulled the sheriff's department parking decal from under the front seat and placed it on the dashboard.

Dani rushed up the wide front stairs and into the red brick building. She found the front office for the education center, but there wasn't anyone around. "Hello?" Dani walked to the back of the room and yelled louder. "Hello?"

An older woman with frizzy permed hair came out of a side room. "I'm sorry. I was making copies. May I help you?"

Dani introduced herself, showed the woman the boy's photograph, and explained that they needed to speak with him.

"Oh dear. I hope he's not in any trouble."

"No. Not at all."

"Oh, well. That's good. He's been in some trouble in the past."

"So. You know who he is?"

"Oh, yes. His name's Bryant Willis."

"I'll need his address and phone number, please."

The woman sat at a desk and tapped on the computer keyboard. She wrote on a piece of notepaper and handed it to Dani.

"Thank you." Dani asked, "What time will Bryant be here today?"

"Oh, he's here now. Come with me, and I'll take you to Mr. Hunt's classroom. That's where Bryant is."

Dani followed the woman down a short hallway. They stopped at the last door on the left. The woman knocked on the door and poked her head inside. "Excuse me, Mr. Hunt. We need Bryant, please." A few seconds later, Bryant stepped out into the hall, and the woman went back to the office.

Dani recognized the boy from the Justice Center camera footage. She introduced herself. "We'd like you to come to our office and give us a description of the man that asked you to deliver the envelope to our office."

"Technically, he didn't ask me. He paid me fifty bucks to deliver it."

Dani didn't respond to that. Instead, she asked, "Would you like your parents to be there when we speak with you?"

"I live in a foster home. Nobody there'll care."

Dani handed Bryant her cell phone. "Call anyway and let them know that we'll give you a ride back to school when you're through."

Bryant shrugged. "Whatever." He handed the phone back to Dani after he disconnected.

"Do you have a backpack or anything?"

"Nope."

"Okay. Let's go then."

Dani and Bryant walked back to her vehicle, stopping by the office to check him out of school.

"What's this all about?" Bryant asked as Dani drove.

"I can't tell you the details."

"The guy did something bad, didn't he?"

Dani didn't answer.

"He was creepy."

"How so?"

Bryant was quiet for a few seconds. Then he shrugged. "I
don't know. His eyes and voice were like… dead. I don't know
how to explain it."

Dani nodded. "I understand what you mean." She parked the
SUV in the Justice Center's lot and led the boy inside. Clearly
excited, Bryant rubbernecked as they walked down the hall to the
detectives' office.

"Wait here." Dani went inside the room. Powers, Verity, and
Webb were still out, and Richards was watching video footage on
his computer. She turned all the whiteboards around to face the
wall. Dani went back out to the hall. "Come on in."

Bryant followed Dani to her desk, taking in everything in the
room. "So, how does this work? Does a sketch artist ask me
questions?"

"We don't have a sketch artist," Dani said. "Too expensive.
We use facial composite software. You select facial features from

a database, and they're blended together to produce a composite image."

Bryant grinned. "That's dope."

Dani pulled a second chair up in front of her desk and indicated for him to sit. Bryant eagerly sat on the chair, facing the computer.

Dani logged into the software program and began asking Bryant questions about Michael. She started with height and weight.

Bryant said, "Oh, man. I don't know how to tell that stuff."

"Can you be general? Was he thin or heavy? Tall or short?"

Bryant shrugged. "He was a regular guy."

Dani nodded, then asked, "What about hair color, length, and style?"

"It was brown. Straight."

Dani adjusted the picture until Bryant felt the hair looked right.

"What about eye color and shape?"

"He was wearing mirror sunglasses," Bryant said. "So, I didn't see his eyes."

"Okay. Then, let's get his glasses."

They continued to work for over an hour until they had an image of Michael.

"Did you see any tattoos or rings on his fingers?"

Bryant thought for a second. "Not that I can remember."

"What about scars?"

Bryant considered this for a few moments, then shook his head. "Didn't see any."

"What about his voice? Anything unusual? An accent?"

"Just creepy. Like I told you before."

Dani thanked Bryant for his help and led him to Connie's desk. "Connie, please have a patrol officer take Bryant back to school."

"That's it?" Bryant asked Dani. "Can I stay and watch you guys work? This is a blast."

Connie said, "This isn't a game, young man!"

Bryant had the good grace to hang his head and mumble, "Sorry, ma'am."

"If we need anything else, we'll contact you," Dani said. "Thanks again." Dani went back to her office and printed off the final image of Michael. Dani straightened the pen, highlighter, and pad of paper on her desk. She rolled her neck right, left, and up, then down.

"You okay?" Emmerson Wilson asked, walking into the office.

Dani looked up. "Fine."

"I heard back from our cell carrier," Wilson said. "The two calls you received were made from different prepaid cell phones. Both went dark immediately after the call ended."

"What does that mean?"

"The guy probably destroyed them." Wilson shrugged. "I would if it were me." With that, he left the room.

Powers and Verity returned to the office within a minute of each other. Powers slumped down onto his desk chair and ran his hand over his hair. "None of the people that live in the area where Josie's body was left saw a thing."

Verity pulled a small notepad out of his shirt pocket. He flipped a few pages, then read from it. "One older woman, Mrs. Yolanda Combs, heard a car stop across the street around eight that morning. She's not sure about the exact time. Mrs. Combs looked out of her bedroom window and saw a man walking away from the car. He was heading north. She's also not sure what he looked like. Her eyesight's not very good. Mrs. Combs is sure that the man was white and had on a sweatshirt, but that's all." Verity slipped the notepad back into his pocket.

"I found that kid," Dani said. She handed Powers and Verity a copy of the sketch. "It's not great, but it's a start."

Webb walked in and said, "Dayton Cooke identified all the remaining calls on Josie's cell log. They were work related." He sat down at the desk he was temporarily occupying.

Verity looked at Richards and asked, "Have you found anything so far?"

Richards shook his head. "I'm still going through the footage of this building. I haven't seen a man with the same body traits as the guy that left the notes for Dani. I'm slogging through it, but it's slow going."

Webb said, "Unless you have something else for me to do, boss, I can help with the video footage."

Verity nodded. "Richards, divide the footage with Webb. We need to finish looking through it as soon as possible." Verity paced between his table and the whiteboards. "Let's review what we know. We know that Mrs. Aiken left for work at seven thirty but never arrived."

Suddenly, Dani jumped up and hurried over to the back wall of the office. She pulled off a Kalispell street map that was taped there. Dani attached the map to a whiteboard and pushed it to the front of the room. "Josie probably took the same route to work every day." Dani studied the map for a few seconds. "From her house, there would only be one way to get downtown." Dani tapped the map. "She'd have to take Evergreen to Whitefish Stage Road." Dani picked up the yellow highlighter off of her desk and marked the roads on the map. "We need to see if there are any cameras along this route." Dani leaned into the map and pointed. "There's a market right there. They might have a camera. Josie would have driven right past the store."

Powers said, "We can also check CCTV cameras in the areas where Josie's car and body were left. Also, the roads in and out of both."

Verity said, "Let's get all the footage between seven thirty and when the body was discovered. Webb and Powers, you can both work that after you finish the footage of this building. It's going to take some time to look at it all. Detective McKenna, you drive the route Mrs. Aiken would have taken to work and see what you can find."

Dani gathered her coat and handbag and hurried outside. She quickly drove the route that Josie would have taken to get home from her office. When she got to the Aiken's house, she made a U-turn and started back toward town.

Dani stopped at the market that she'd seen on the map. She walked around the building and saw that there was no surveillance camera. Dani got back in her Jeep and slowly drove along the route that Josie would have taken. A car came up behind her and began tailgating and honking. Dani ignored it and continued scanning the buildings along the road. She turned off the street onto the driveway of the first business she came to. Revving his car's engine, the driver behind her sped past, once more honking. Dani circled the building. There weren't any cameras.

The next business Dani came to was a mini-storage facility. Each of the four rows of storage buildings had one camera at the end of the row. All of the cameras were pointed toward the street. "Yes!" Dani said, slapping the steering wheel with the palm of her hand. She drove back to the front entrance and parked. Dani went inside and introduced herself to the teenage boy sitting behind the counter. "I need to see your video footage for Tuesday morning." The boy leaned back in his rickety wooden chair and yelled at a closed door next to the counter. "Dad!"

A very skinny man with long greasy hair came out of the door. "What?"

Dani saw that the man was missing a front tooth. She introduced herself again, held up her badge, and repeated her request.

"Do you got a warrant?" the man asked.

Dani leaned one elbow on the counter. "No. Do I need one? Because I could have one here in less than an hour. Then I would want to look at all the records for the place. Payroll. Taxes." Dani shrugged. "Everything."

The man squinted at Dani for a second, then turned toward the teenager. "Johnny, get the video for Tuesday morning."

The boy shrugged. "Okay." He tapped keys the keyboard that sat on the desk behind the counter. Dani saw that Johnny had been playing a video game on the computer. He opened a separate window on the monitor so that he didn't have to close the game. Johnny tapped on the keyboard some more. "What time?"

"Seven thirty."

"Here ya' go."

Dani moved around the counter and stood beside Johnny. The desk was filthy, so she didn't touch it. Dani bent at the waist and leaned in. The video was date and time stamped. There were four cameras, and the monitor was split into four screens. Johnny tapped a key, and the videos started playing. The street could be seen clearly on the first camera. Dani watched the videos until the time showed as eight thirty. There was no sign of Josie's car. Dani stood and looked out the side window at the street.

"You done?" Johnny asked.

"I need to take that video with me."

Johnny looked questioningly at his father. "Should I give it to her?"

"Yeah, go ahead."

~~~

Dani didn't get home that night until almost nine. She greeted Bo and poured the rest of the open bottle of Chardonnay into a glass. She took it with her as she walked through the house, checking all the locks. When Dani finished, she sat on the sofa and sipped her wine. Bo curled up on the floor, laying his head on her left foot. Dani removed her Glock and cell phone from their holsters and set them on the coffee table. She leaned her head on the back of the couch and closed her eyes. Dani was contemplating how fate seemed to favor the bad as often as the good when her cell phone rang.

Even though Dani knew her calls were now being monitored, she turned on her recorder. Dani had placed it on the end table in the living room before leaving for work that morning. She'd wanted to be prepared, not taken by surprise as she had been when Michael called the first time.

Dani answered in a voice that she hoped was devoid of all emotion. "Michael."

"Why Dani, I'm honored that you know it's me."

"Don't flatter yourself," Dani said. "The caller ID showed as unknown. You're the only person that calls me on burner phones."

"You shouldn't be rude to me," Michael said. "It makes me angry. Which... is... not... good."

Dani's heart thumped like it was trying to break out of her chest. Even though Dani wasn't sure she wanted to know the answer, she asked, "Why me?"

"Because you're special to me."

Dani asked, "Why?"

"Because of our special connection."

"What connection is that?"

"Oh come on," Michael said. "Don't play dumb. You know what I'm talking about."

Fear wrapped its tendrils around Dani. Bo sat up and started to growl.

"I'll let you get some rest now," Michael said. "Goodnight, Dani. I love you."

Dani rushed to the bathroom and threw up into the toilet. Beneath her shirt, sweat trickled down her sides and back. Bo stood in the doorway, whining. Dani's cell phone rang in the living room. She rinsed her mouth out in the bathroom sink and hurried to answer the phone. She saw that it was Powers. "McKenna."

"Another burner," Powers said. "Not surprisingly, when patrol got to the location, Michael was gone." Powers paused. "You okay?"

"I'm fine," Dani said. "You don't need to worry about me."

"Okay. Try to get some sleep."

"Good night." Dani set the phone on the coffee table. She reached into the front pocket of her pants and pulled out two Xanax pills. Dani washed them down with wine. She sat on the couch and slowly drank the rest of the wine in her glass. Then, she stood and walked through the house checking all of the locks and making sure the security system was armed.

CHAPTER 5

Dani woke to shafts of morning light filtering through the thick canopy of trees surrounding her house. She realized that she'd fallen asleep on the couch after drinking an entire bottle of wine. Her head was pounding, and her mouth was as dry as the desert. Dani showered and dressed for work. She left her hair down so that it could dry as she drove. Before leaving the house, Dani put some Xanax pills in her pocket. She stopped at the same convenience store as she had the previous morning and bought coffee. She drank one as she drove. When Dani walked into the office with the second cup of coffee, she saw that she was the last to arrive.

Powers looked at the dark circles under Dani's eyes and frowned. "You get any sleep last night?"

Dani nodded. "Some."

Connie shuffled into the room. "Mailman just delivered another message." She handed the manila envelope to Dani.

Dani put on latex gloves, opened the envelope, and put the enclosed items in protective sleeves. Then, she read the typed note out loud. "Dearest Dani, The bible says, 'A man or a woman who acts as a medium or clairvoyant shall be put to death.' I look forward to talking to you again soon. Love, Michael." She studied the two photographs that had been in the manila envelope. Like Josie, the woman in the newest pictures looked to be in her late twenties. She had long blonde hair, a straight nose, full lips, and startling blue eyes. The first photograph was again a close-up of the woman's face. The second was from a distance and showed the woman walking on a sidewalk. She was wearing a suit and high heels. She had a slim figure and shapely legs.

Connie left the room shaking her head and mumbling, "Dear Lord. Poor, poor dears."

Looking at the manila envelope, Dani said, "The postal stamp's from the Bigfork Post Office. For it to get here today, Michael would have needed to mail it two days ago."

"It's hard not to appreciate good planning," Powers said. "Even if it is by some sicko."

Dani said, "Nobody's ever arrested for murder, they're only arrested for not planning it properly." She took the note and photographs and made a copy of each. Dani attached them to a whiteboard and wheeled it to the front of the room.

Verity sat on the edge of the table he was using as a desk. "When this type of murderer chooses a victim there's a trait that the killer finds attractive. That trait will be common among all the victims. It's termed the Ideal Victim Type. The murderer selects a victim he considers the right type. Someone he can control, either through manipulation or strength. Once he's found a victim that's ideal, he'll stalk her before acting." Verity paused. "You guys notice anything about the two women in the photographs?"

Richards said, "They could be sisters."

Verity turned toward Dani. "They look like you."

Powers stared at the pictures. "Hell, you're right. They do."

Dani looked at the photographs. "I don't look like them at all."

Webb asked, "You don't see the resemblance?"

Dani shook her head. "No."

Powers said, "Hang on a minute. I have an idea." He took out his cell phone, held it up, and took a close-up of Dani's face. Powers took the phone to his computer, hooked them together with a USB cable, and printed out the photograph. Then, he held it up next to the pictures of the two victims.

Dani studied the photograph of herself. She leaned closer and looked back and forth at the three pictures. A frisson of fear sent a jolt through her body.

Powers asked, "Does that mean he's going to come after Dani?"

"There's no way to know that," Verity said, shaking his head. "He might not want to actually hurt Detective McKenna. But, she's definitely not a stranger to him." Verity stared at Dani. "You definitely know this guy."

"Like I said before... I have no idea who Michael is."

Dani sat at her desk and typed on the computer's keyboard. She stood and wrote 'Leviticus 20:27' below the third note on the whiteboard. Then, she wrote the words 'far-seeing, perceptive, shrewd, intuitive, and fortune teller' on the whiteboard.

Powers read what she'd written. "What are you thinking?"

"Michael interpreted the meaning of a sorceress. Maybe he's doing the same with the word clairvoyant." Dani pointed at the board. "That's the definition." She shrugged. "I'll check online for fortune tellers." Dani typed on her computer's keyboard, then read from the monitor. "Most of these are the over-the-phone kind. There's one local tarot card reader." Dani opened the website and shook her head. "Definitely not the woman in the photographs."

Powers said, "What other kind of jobs are far-seeing, shrewd, and intuitive?"

"Let me look at synonyms again." Dani tapped keys and read aloud. "Magical, diviner, prophesier, brainy." Dani sat back in her chair, thinking. "There's a job that looks ahead wisely and is like a fortune teller... a stock market analyst."

Verity said, "That's a stretch."

Powers frowned at him. "You got any better ideas?"

Dani leaned forward and began typing on the keyboard again. "There are two companies in Whitefish. They both have pictures of their analysts on their website. But, none of them are the woman in the photos." She paused, reading the monitor. "In Kalispell, there's one investment company on Second Street. They don't have pictures of their analysts."

Powers said, "Let's go check it out."

Verity nodded. "That's acceptable to me."

Powers rolled his eyes. "I'm so glad."

Dani grabbed her handbag out of the bottom desk drawer and rushed with Powers outside to their SUV. He started the vehicle and sped out of the parking lot. The detectives arrived at the investment company a few short minutes later. Powers parked on the sidewalk in front of the building. Dani and Powers rushed inside and showed the receptionist their identification. The woman's eyes became the size of silver dollars.

A man dressed in a black suit, a white dress shirt, and a black and white checked tie came out of an office. "I'm Elliot Grey. I'm the manager. How can I help you?"

Dani pulled the copy of the close-up photo of the unidentified woman out of her handbag and handed it to Grey. "Do you know this woman?"

"Of course. That's Terra. Terra Tucker. She's an analyst here. And, she's also my fiancé."

Dani asked, "Is she here?"

Grey shook his head. "She goes to the gym at seven thirty every day before work."

Powers said, "Call her. Now!"

Grey looked back and forth between the two detectives. "What's wrong?" He pulled his cell phone out of a pocket inside his suit coat and tapped on the screen. "It's ringing."

"Tell her to drive straight here," Powers said. "Tell her not to stop for any reason."

"Oh my God," Grey said. "What's going on?"

Dani said, "We'll explain later. Any answer?"

Grey shook his head. "Straight to voicemail."

Dani reached into her handbag and took out a pen and pad of paper. "We need her phone number, home address, and kind of car she's driving." Grey took the paper and pen from Dani, jotted down the information, and handed them back.

Powers asked, "Which gym does she go to?"

"Flathead Fitness." Grey scrubbed his hand down his face. "It's on 2 East."

"Keep calling her!" Powers said as he and Dani rushed out the front door. Powers squealed the tires as he pulled onto Second Street. He hit the lights and siren.

Dani typed the name of the gym into the GPS and said, "Eight minutes." When the detectives arrived, they circled the building looking for Terra's car. They didn't see it. Powers parked in a no parking zone at the front door. The detectives hurried inside, and showed the receptionist their identification and Terra's photograph. "Has this woman been in today?"

The receptionist looked at the photograph. "Terra?" She shook her head. "She hasn't come in yet."

"We're going to look around, just in case," Powers said.

The woman shrugged. "Whatever."

Dani and Powers walked through the workout areas but didn't see Terra. Dani went into the women's locker room and checked the showers and toilet stalls. She shook her head when she came out.

"He has her." Powers slapped the palm of his hand on the wall. "Damn it!" As Powers drove back to the office, Dani radioed dispatch. "We need an APB on a vehicle belonging to Terra Tucker." Dani gave dispatch the make and model of Terra's car and her home address.

The two detectives rushed inside and down the hallway to their office. As Powers updated the FBI agents on the latest missing woman, Dani typed a warrant request for Terra's cell phone. Dani copied the request that she'd used for Josie's cell, changing only the name. She took the paperwork to Connie and asked her to get it upstairs.

Powers called Elliott Grey and updated him on the threat against Terra. Powers also asked Grey for the names and numbers of Terra's friends and family. As they had with Josie, the detectives checked with the jail and hospital. Terra wasn't at either one. Verity, Powers, and Dani divided the list of friends and family, and started the unpleasant process of calling them. When the three had finished, they were certain that Michael had Terra.

Connie came into the room and said, "We got the warrant for Terra Tucker's phone." She handed it to Verity.

Powers said, "That was fast."

"A second young woman's been kidnapped," Connie said. "Judge Bartel promised he'd expedite anythin' you need for this case." As Connie left the office, Dani could hear her reciting some kind of prayer.

Verity pulled a whiteboard to the front of the room. He said, "Let's review the timeline for Mrs. Aiken's kidnapping again. Perhaps that will give us some insight on Ms. Tucker." Verity started writing. "Mrs. Aiken disappeared just after seven thirty Tuesday morning. Michael delivered the note here at seven-fifty that morning. He turned her phone back on at ten Thursday morning. Michael had Mrs. Aiken for over forty-eight hours before he killed her."

Powers said, "I'm not so sure I want to know this, Verity. But, what do you think he does to the women in the time that he has them?"

"In the case of an organized lust murderer like Michael, there will be sexual assault and torture."

Dani closed her eyes, trying to keep unbidden images from entering her mind.

"I was right." Powers stood and began pacing between the sets of desks. "I didn't want to know."

Dani opened her eyes and voiced an idea that had popped into her head. "Maybe Michael was already in Josie's car when she got into it Tuesday morning." Dani went to the street map on the whiteboard and looked at the different routes from Josie's house to the Justice Center. "If Michael drove from Josie's house to the Center in her car that would explain why it didn't go past the storage place. It also explains how he made it here twenty minutes after Josie left her house. And, he was seen walking away from Josie's car, so he must have left his own vehicle close enough to walk to."

Powers said, "When Michael abandoned Josie's car, we know she wasn't with him. So, where did he leave her while he drove her car here, dropped off the note, drove her car to the church, walked to his car, and drove back to where he'd left her?"

Dani said, "In his vehicle."

Powers stopped and pointed at Dani. "That's it. Has to be. It's the only way the timing works."

Verity sat on his chair, placed his elbows on the table, and tented his fingers under his chin. "Michael kidnapped Terra before she made it to the gym. So, he was either in Terra's car when she left home like you said, or he somehow got her to stop on the way. Michael couldn't have grabbed Terra in front of the gym. There are too many people around."

Powers sat back and rubbed his hair. "Terra's phone's dead, so we can't trace it. We have patrol out looking everywhere. What the hell else can we do to find her?"

Verity said, "Perhaps there's some connection between the two women. Gym, church, dry cleaners. Anywhere Michael could have found the two women. Other than randomly on the street. I'll call Mrs. Aiken's husband and Ms. Tucker's fiancé to explore that."

"We have the warrant for Terra's cell," Dani said. "We can check both women's contacts and call logs to see if any of them match."

It took two hours for Dani and Powers to compare the information on the two women's phones. "Hell," Powers said, shaking his head. "No matches."

Verity was on the phone. He hung up and said, "I talked to both the husband and fiancé. There doesn't seem to be any apparent connection between Mrs. Aiken and Ms. Tucker."

Dani asked, "So, Michael took them purely because of how they look?"

Verity nodded. "That would verify the ideal victim theory. He picked them because they look like you."

Dani cringed. Her skin crawled and her stomach knotted at the thought that she was the cause of the two women being targeted. "So, now what?" she asked. "We have no leads. Nothing to help us find Terra before Michael murders her. What can we do?"

Verity looked at Dani. "Last night Michael said you two have a special connection. Any idea what he's talking about?"

Dani shook her head. "No."

Verity said, "Well, the obvious course of action is to dig into your life. Your friends, acquaintances, anything that might help lead us to Michael."

Dani scowled, shaking her head. "No way. My private life is just that."

"Not anymore," Verity said. "Michael is in it. Somehow, somewhere."

Powers said, "Dani leads a very solitary life."

"Good," Verity said. "That will make it much faster and easier for us to identify potential suspects."

Dani crossed her arms over her chest. "I'm not okay with having my life examined like this."

113

Verity walked over to the last whiteboard and tapped the photo of Terra. "This woman's life could depend on it. I would think that's a small price to pay." Verity paused. "Unless you have something to hide."

Powers said to Dani, "I hate to agree with him, but he's right. So, suck it up and help Terra."

Dani moved the pen on her desktop a millimeter to the left. "Alright. I need a couple of minutes before we start." She walked down the hall to the bathroom, breathing deeply in an attempt to remain calm. Once inside, Dani pulled two Xanax pills from her pants pocket and swallowed them dry. Dani leaned against the bathroom wall and closed her eyes. She felt like her life was circling the drain.

Connie pushed open the bathroom door, almost hitting Dani with it. Dani quickly stood straight and faked a small smile. She walked back to the office and sat at her desk with a sigh. "Where do we start?"

Verity wrote 'Family' on a whiteboards.

Dani recited the names of her birth father and mother and the year her father had died.

"Stepfather's name?" Verity asked, marker in hand, poised to write on the board.

"Dominic Riordan."

Verity dropped his hand to his side. "Your stepfather's Dominic Riordan?!"

Dani inhaled deeply, then exhaled. "Yep."

Powers looked confused. "Who is he?"

Verity said, "One of the wealthiest men in the state. He owns and is the president of Garrett Mining in Missoula. The company's worth around fifty million dollars."

This drew the attention of both Richards and Webb. Richards whistled and said, "Holy crap."

Powers looked at Dani. "Why the hell didn't I know this?"

"Because people react like all of you are right now," Dani said. "Besides, I haven't spoken to him in twelve years."

Verity asked, "Why not?"

Dani said, "I can't see why that would matter."

"Let me decide whether it's relative or not," Verity said.

"We had a falling out. I went to live with my grandmother the summer after I was a junior in high school. I lived with her until she died seven years ago. That was right after I graduated from college."

The squeaking sound of the marker moving across the board broke the silence in the room. Verity asked, "Are you in touch with your mother?"

"Again. I can't see why that would matter. But... no. I'm not."

Verity asked, "Any siblings?"

"One stepbrother. The company's named after him."

"Are you in communication with him?"

"Yes."

Verity wrote 'Garrett Riordan' on the whiteboard. "Now, let's list your friends."

Dani was silent for a few seconds, then she said, "I don't have any." She looked down and straightened the marker on her desktop.

Verity made a note on the whiteboard, then asked, "What about acquaintances outside of work?"

Dani didn't have to pause to think. "Only Damian Moss. He's been my trainer and sparring partner for the past seven years."

Irving wrote the name on the board and circled it.

Dani shook her head. "Damian doesn't fit the physical characteristics. He's too short and muscled."

116

"Those could be off by a considerable margin."

Powers shook his head. "No. Dani and I saw Michael on this building's footage. He's tall and slim. The opposite of Moss."

Verity said, "I'm not eliminating him on that alone." He paused. "Let's go through the list of colleagues that you have day-to-day contact with." Verity wrote as Dani and Powers said names. When they were finished, he circled Powers' and Howland's names.

Powers' face turned red. "Seriously?!"

Verity said, "Nobody can be eliminated just because they work here. One thing I've learned from this job is that there can be evil in all of us."

Dani pinched the bridge of her nose. She felt a stress headache coming on. "I hate this."

"Yes, we know," Verity said in a disinterested tone. "Okay, let's start with Damian Moss. Dani, you take him. Powers, you take Howland. And, I'll take Powers." Verity paused. "I'll inform Corporal Tirrell about what we're doing and why. He's going to need to apprise the district attorney."

Powers shot Verity a look that could thaw an iceberg. "What are we supposed to search for during this fishing expedition?"

Verity pulled over another whiteboard and began making a list as he talked. "Growing up in a home where substances were abused. Emotional abuse or neglect when a child. Violent events during childhood. Any complaints of voyeurism or animal cruelty as a child. Behavioral problems at a young age. Social isolation. Anti-social tendencies. Self-control issues. Also, look into any head injuries received during accidents. Seventy percent of serial killers received extensive head injuries as children or adolescents."

Powers upper lip had retreated until it was tight across his teeth. "Let me save you some time, Verity. None of those apply to me."

Dani said, "What did you just tell me? Suck it up."

Powers took a deep breath. "Yeah. Okay. But, that doesn't make it any less annoying."

"Tell me about it," Dani said. "I'm pretty sure I'm not going to have a sparring partner after this."

Powers said, "She has a point. We can ask the people we speak with to keep quiet, but in all likelihood, they're not going to. And, we're not going to make any friends here."

"One of the consequences of the job," Verity said. "If Michael follows the same pattern, we have about forty hours to save Terra."

118

An hour later, Dani said, "I've finished my online stalking of Damian."

Verity moved to the whiteboard to make notes.

"There's only one person for me to talk to about Damian. His mother. Damian's father died last year, and he's an only child. He has Facebook and Twitter accounts for his business, but no personal accounts. So, I can't find anything about a girlfriend or friends." Dani took her handbag out of the drawer. "I'm headed to Damian's mother's house."

Powers said, "Be careful out there."

In the parking lot, Dani took the keychain out of her handbag. Before she unlocked the door to her Jeep, Dani looked in the back window to make sure someone wasn't hiding inside. When she saw that the SUV was empty, she climbed into the driver's seat. Closing and locking the door, Dani entered Moss' mother's home address into the vehicle's GPS.

As Dani drove, thoughts ricocheted around in her head. When Dani had looked at the list of people in her life, she'd realized that she was alone, marooned on her own private island of fear and distrust.

Doctor Ellison's words from twelve years ago unexpectedly made themselves heard, like they knew their time had come. "If you want to be free, all you have to do is let go."

"Yeah, well," Dani said out loud. "That's a whole lot easier said than done."

"At the next intersection, make a U-turn." The console GPS repeated, "Make a U-turn."

Dani shook her head to clear it of cobwebs from the past, and turned the Jeep around in the middle of the street. She parked on Tenth Street, in front of Moss' mother's house. Dani saw that it was small, with a dark brown metal roof and white siding. The trim around the windows, as well as the front door, were painted pale blue.

After climbing out of the Jeep, Dani pressed the lock button two times on the key fob. As she walked to the front door of the house, she unconsciously pushed it once more. The horn blared in response. Dani walked up the front steps, which were flanked by white and red petunias. The bright blooms were in direct opposition to Dani's mood.

Dani rang the doorbell and waited. A stylishly dressed woman with wavy white hair answered the front door. She asked, "May I help you?"

Dani held up her badge. "Flathead County Sheriff's Detective." Dani intentionally didn't give her name. "Are you Mrs. Moss?"

"Yes."

"I need to ask you some questions about your son, Damian. May I come in?"

Mrs. Moss stepped back to allow Dani to enter. "Come into the living room." Mrs. Moss sat in a tan leather wingchair and indicated for Dani to sit on the dark brown upholstered sofa. "What's this about?" she asked.

"I need to ask you some general questions about your son."

"Like what?" Mrs. Moss asked, frowning.

Dani pulled a notepad and pen out of her handbag. "About Damian's childhood."

"Such as?"

"Did he have any social problems as a child?"

Mrs. Moss looked Dani in the eye, then stood. "I don't mean to be rude, Detective. But, I would like my attorney to be present when I answer any questions you have about my son." Mrs. Moss walked back to the front door and once more held it open.

Dani thanked Mrs. Moss for her time, retracing her steps back to the Jeep. Dani again checked in the back before she opened the driver's door. She drove back the way she'd come only ten minutes prior. Walking into the office, she said to Verity,

"Damian's mother completely shut me down." Dani sat at her desk and stowed her handbag. "Where's Powers?"

"He went to talk to Howland's ex-wife."

Dani said, "I didn't know Tate had been married."

Verity watched Dani for a reaction as he asked, "Anything between you two?"

"What? No. Absolutely not."

"Well, he's definitely interested in you," Verity said. "I saw him watching you as you drove out of the parking lot."

Webb looked up from the computer screen he'd been staring into and said, "That's a little creepy."

Richards smirked and said, "Or maybe he has it bad for Dani."

She shook her head. "That's ridiculous."

Verity walked over to the whiteboard and wrote 'divorced six years ago' and 'no children' below Howland's name.

Dani's cell phone rang. She looked at the screen. "It's Damian. That didn't take long." She swiped the answer icon.

Before Dani could say anything, Moss asked, "Was that you at my mom's?"

"Yes."

"What's going on?" Moss asked.

"We have a murder case where the perp's contacting me. We're investigating everyone that I interact with on a regular basis. It's nothing personal."

"That's not how it feels," Moss said. "After all these years, I thought you trusted me."

"It's not about that. We're even looking at my partner." Dani paused. "I'm just doing my job."

"Yeah? Well, I can't do my job with someone who doesn't trust me."

"I understand. I'm sorry."

"Goodbye, Dani." Moss disconnected the call.

Dani sighed. "Well, that's one less person in my life."

Powers walked into the office. "Howland's ex said he's a great guy." Powers sat on his desk chair with a loud sigh. "She had an affair. Said Howland was upset, but never violent." Powers removed a small notebook from his shirt pocket, flipped it open, and read. "Ex said Howland never got past it. They even went to counseling. Howland filed for divorce a year later. Ex said the divorce was amicable and Howland was generous to her. I got the impression that she'd gladly get back together if he would go for it."

The black marker squeaked as Verity made notes on the whiteboard below Howland's name. "Talk to anyone else?"

"Parents are dead. He has one younger sister, who lives in the Seattle area. I left a message for her to call me back. Didn't mention what it was about."

Verity said to Powers, "I spoke to your two sisters on the phone." Verity raised his bushy eyebrows. "I was surprised that they were so willing to answer my questions about you."

Powers said, "That's because there's nothing to tell."

"It does seem that way," Verity said. "I'm going to eliminate you as a suspect."

Powers sarcastically said, "Gee. Thanks so much."

Verity continued unfazed. "For now, Moss is our prime suspect."

Dani rubbed her forehead. "It can't be Damian. He doesn't fit the physical profile."

Verity said, "I'll request that Tirrell assign a patrol unit to shadow Moss. Powers, we need a warrant to search Moss' home, work, and vehicle."

Powers shook his head. "Okay. I'll get a request upstairs. But, I agree with Dani. This is a waste of time."

Richards interrupted by yawning. He rubbed his eyes and said, "I need a break from this. I'm going to get coffee. Anyone want some?"

Verity shook his head and stood. He walked out of the room and down the hall towards the sheriff's office.

Dani answered Richards. "I could use a large coffee. Cream and sugar, please."

Powers shook his head. "I've had my ration for the day."

Webb stood and stretched. "I'll go with you. My old body can't take all this sitting."

Verity returned and sat on his chair. He placed his elbows on the table and laced his fingers together. Verity looked up at Dani. "I explained to Corporal Tirrell why I believe that you're hiding something. Or lying."

Powers swiveled his chair toward Verity. "You did what?!"

Verity said, "The sheriff agrees with me."

Powers shook his head. "You're a piece of work."

Dani suddenly felt physically and mentally exhausted. She didn't know whether it was due to Damian's phone call or Verity's continual harassment. She rubbed her forehead. "I don't know anything that could help Terra."

"You might think that this secret of yours isn't related to what's happening to these women," Verity said. "But you're not the one that should be making that call."

Dani pulled the top drawer of her desk open and removed the bottle of ibuprofen that she kept inside. She shook two into her hand, stood, and walked out of the office. Dani went down the hall to the women's restroom and swallowed the pills with water from the faucet. She went into one of the stalls and locked the door. Dani sat on the toilet seat and put her head in her hands. She sat like that until she had the energy to stand up and rejoin the fray.

While Dani was gone, Powers had taken the warrant request upstairs. He walked back into the office and said, "Connie was right. Judge Bartel had me wait while he signed the warrant."

Verity practically sprang from his chair. "Good." He took the warrant out of Powers' hand and said, "We'll start at Moss' business."

Powers said, "Dani and I'll meet you there." The detectives went out to the parking lot and got into their SUV. As Powers drove, he radioed dispatch and asked that a patrol deputy meet them at the boxing studio.

The two detectives waited by the front door for Verity and the deputy. After they arrived, Powers tried the front door. It was locked. He pounded on the dented metal with his fist. Powers waited a few seconds, then banged even louder. The door vibrated with each thump. When Moss opened the door, Powers handed him the warrant. "Damian Moss, this is a warrant to search these premises, your home, and your vehicle."

Moss looked confused. Seeing Dani, he asked her, "What's going on?"

Powers said, "We're not at liberty to discuss ongoing investigations."

Todd Nash was the officer that had been tagged for the search. He approached Moss.

Powers said, "Mr. Moss, please wait outside with this deputy." Powers and Verity moved inside the building.

As Dani passed Moss, he said to her, "You know I couldn't have done whatever this is about. You know me."

Dani said, "I really am sorry." She walked past Moss, blood rushing in her ears. Dani felt nauseous and light headed.

Powers, Dani, and Verity gathered together a few feet inside the building. Dani removed latex gloves from a pocket on the side of her pants and handed a pair to both men.

Verity said, "In this type of murder, the killer often takes a souvenir from his victim as a reminder. So, keep an eye out for women's jewelry and underwear. That type of thing."

As the space was completely open, except for one small office and bathroom, the search only took forty-five minutes. They found a woman's bra, a pair of flip-flops, and a pink sweater in a box labeled 'Lost and Found'. Dani bagged and tagged all three. Then, she logged them on an evidence sheet.

When the three exited the building, Powers said to Moss, "We're going to need the keys to your house and truck."

Moss pulled a set of keys out of his pocket. He removed two keys from the ring and handed them to Powers.

Verity said, "I'll stay here and search the truck while you and Dani search the house."

Powers nodded. "Nash, I'd appreciate it if you'd see that Mr. Moss stays where he is until we've completed the searches."

Nash nodded. "Will do."

Dani and Powers rode in silence the short distance to Moss' home on Fifth Avenue. The house had tan siding and an asphalt shingled roof. A pot of purple petunias sat on a wooden stool next to the front door. Dani wondered if Moss' mother had given him the flowers.

Powers opened the front door with the key that Moss had given to him. The detectives stepped into a cramped living room with matching dark brown upholstered furniture. An arched doorway led into the kitchen. The cabinets had been painted pale blue, and the white appliances were old but clean. There were two narrow bedrooms off of the kitchen, one on each side of the hall that ended at a small bathroom. The house didn't have a laundry room or a garage. The only decorations on the walls were posters of different types of martial arts, including aikido, taekwondo, wrestling, and boxing. These had been stuck on the walls with clear pushpins.

The detectives found access to the attic in one of the bedrooms. Powers said, "I'll give you a leg up so you can take a look in there."

Dani placed her right foot in Powers cupped hands. As he lifted her, Dani pushed aside the piece of plywood covering the opening. She grabbed the sides and stuck her head in. Dani looked all around the attic space, then said, "Nothing but insulation and wires."

Powers lowered her to the floor. "Let's start searching for any female items or something showing a place that Moss might have taken the women."

The detectives each took a bedroom, then converged in the kitchen and searched it together. It only took Dani a few minutes to look through the bathroom. When they had finished the living room, Powers said, "There's nothing here."

Dani said, "That's because we're looking at the wrong guy."

"I agree. Come on, let's head back to the studio." When Powers pulled up, Nash and Moss were still standing out front. It looked like Verity had completed his search of the truck because he was anxiously pacing on the sidewalk.

When Verity saw the detectives' vehicle, he rushed over to Powers' window. Leaning forward at the waist, he said, "The truck had been cleaned recently. Or, Moss keeps it that way."

Dani said, "His house was neat and clean, too. We didn't find any evidence in it."

Verity said, "I contacted Corporal Tirrell and told him that it would be prudent to keep Moss under surveillance, as he's the most likely suspect that we have. The sheriff agreed. As Deputy Nash is here, Corporal Tirrell assigned him to take the first shift."

Powers shook his head. "Okay... but Dani and I both think it's a waste of resources."

Verity turned, walked to his rental car, and drove off.

Powers gave Moss his keys back and told him he was free to go. Powers thanked Nash for his help and went back to the SUV, where Dani was waiting.

When the detectives walked into their office a few minutes later, they found Tirrell there, talking to Verity.

The sheriff said, "The press got ahold of some details about Josie Aiken's murder from her husband."

Powers rubbed his hand over his hair. "That's just great."

Tirrell said, "Reporter from the local station called me. Wanted to know if I had a comment. I hung up and went right to the editor-in-chief in New York City. Explained how important it is to our investigation that no details are leaked. I got him to agree to wait until after our press conference tomorrow morning to run what they have."

Powers asked, "What press conference?"

"Connie set it up for nine o'clock in the morning," Tirrell said. "Agent Verity asked me to take the lead since we're the local agency. The two of you need to be there, so the public has faces to put with the investigators." When the detectives both nodded, Tirrell said, "Agent Verity believes there's nothing else you can do tonight to find Terra. I'm ordering you to go home."

After Dani and Powers nodded a second time, Tirrell and Verity walked out of the room together. The detectives could hear the sound of their footsteps moving down the hallway toward the front doors.

Powers shook his head. "I don't understand why Tirrell doesn't see Verity for the ass that he is."

Dani shook her head. "Beats me."

Powers said, "Come on. I'll walk out with you."

As they made their way to the parking lot, Dani said, "I can't stand the thought of doing nothing while Terra's out there."

"I don't know about you, but I don't have any more ideas about how to find her. Unfortunately, I think Verity's right. There's nothing we can do tonight."

Dani sighed. "I guess you're right."

Powers veered off toward his vehicle. "See you in the morning."

"Good night." Dani waited for Powers to drive out of the parking lot. Then, she checked to make sure that nobody was around. Dani turned on the light on her cell and looked inside her Jeep. Seeing that nobody was there, she clicked the fob to unlock the door. Dani heard footsteps behind her. She turned and saw that Tate Howland was approaching.

Howland walked swiftly to Dani's Jeep. He said, "I wanted to see how you're doing. Any more panic attacks?"

"No."

"You look worn out. When was the last time you ate?"

Dani attempted a smile. "Does cream and sugar in coffee count?"

Howland chuckled. "Definitely not."

Dani pulled the Jeep's door open. "Thanks for checking on me." She climbed inside and drove away.

Howland watched Dani until he couldn't see her Jeep anymore. Then, he went back upstairs to his office and locked it up for the night.

~~~

Dani made sure the dog feeder still had food in it. She took a chilled bottle of Chardonnay out of the refrigerator and opened it. Dani filled a large wine glass, started a vinyl album playing, and settled into the couch. She took a Xanax pill out of her pants pocket and swallowed it with a mouth full of wine. Dani closed her eyes and let the soft classical music soothe her frayed nerves. Before the first song had finished, Bo stood up from where he'd been laying on the floor and started to growl.

Dani's eyes flew open. She jumped up and drew her Glock out of its holster. Dani took the safety off. "What is it, boy?" Bo's hackle stood up on his back. He trotted over to the front door and started to bark, deep and loud.

When the doorbell chimed, Dani's heart began to race. She held her Glock ready in her right hand and looked through the peephole. Tate Howland was standing on the porch. Dani quieted Bo, disarmed the security system, and opened the door. "What are you doing here?"

Tate held up a large pizza box and smiled, causing his dimples to show prominently on his face. "Best pizza in town."

"How did you know where I live?"

"I got your address from work, of course."

"Of course."

"I was concerned about you," Tate said. "I wanted to help." He shrugged. "Figured food wouldn't be a bad thing."

"Well, you're here now. You might as well come in."

Tate stepped inside. "Who's this?" he asked, reaching out to pet Bo. The dog growled a warning, and Tate jerked his hand back.

Dani locked the front door and rearmed the alarm. She patted the dog's side. "This is Bo. He's my guardian."

Tate nodded. "Good. I'm glad to know your safe way out here." He walked to the kitchen and set the pizza on the island. "Where are your plates?"

"I'll get them," Dani said, holstering her Glock. She removed two plates from inside one of the kitchen cabinets and placed them on the island. Then, Dani took two sets of flatware and two dark green cloth napkins out of a drawer and set them next to the plates.

Tate opened the pizza box. "I got all meat. Figured that as slim as you are, you wouldn't care about the calories."

Dani's stomach growled loudly. She blushed and said, "I have Chardonnay if you'd like some."

"Thanks. That would be great."

Dani poured a glass of wine from the open bottle and set it on the island. She went into the living room, retrieved her glass, and refilled it.

Tate put two large pieces of pizza on a plate and handed it to Dani. She took it, the glass of wine, and a napkin to the living room. Dani sat in one of the armchairs. Tate sat on the couch. Bo positioned himself between the two, never taking his eyes off of Tate.

As they ate, Tate looked around the great room. "Your home's beautiful. As I drove up, I saw the amazing view you have."

"Thanks," Dani said. "I like it."

"How did you ever find this place?"

"It was my grandmother's home. She left it to me when she died." Dani paused. "I spent a lot of time here during holidays and the summer."

"I'm sorry to hear about her passing," Tate said. "It sounds like the two of you were close."

Dani was quiet for a few seconds. Then she said, "We were. Without her, I probably wouldn't be alive." Dani stood and went back to the kitchen. She brought back the bottle of wine and filled both glasses.

Lightning strikes cracked open the evening sky and thunder exploded across the mountain peaks. Dani and Tate could see rain falling in the shafts of light from the moon.

Dani covered her mouth with her hand as a yawn threatened. She looked at her watch. "It's late, and I'm exhausted. Thanks for bringing the pizza by."

Tate got the not so subtle hint. He gathered the dishes and set them on the kitchen counter, next to the sink. Tate said good night to Dani and goodbye to Bo.

Dani disarmed the security system and unlocked the front door. After Tate walked outside, she relocked the door and rearmed the alarm. Then, Dani checked that the rest of the doors and windows in the house were locked. She added more wine to her glass and went back to the living room.

Dani jumped when her cell phone rang. Bo growled in response. Dani pulled the phone out of the holder on her belt and looked at the caller identification. She turned on the recorder and put the phone on speaker. "Michael."

"You had a visitor this evening. A man." Michael enunciated each of his next five words. "I do not like that."

"He's a man I work with. All we did was eat pizza."

There was silence for a few seconds before Michael said, "That's good. Because I know you've been saving yourself for me. Don't do anything to ruin what we have."

"What are you talking about? What do we have?"

"You know we have a special bond. I love you, Dani. Good night." Michael ended the call.

Dani sat on the couch and propped her elbows on her knees. Memories of the past swam through her mind. Dani tried to focus on the sound of the rain to still her thoughts, but it didn't work. She stood and paced back and forth in the living room. When Dani's phone rang again, she looked at the caller identification and saw that it was Powers. She swiped the answer icon and said, "Hey."

Powers said, "No luck with the trace. Michael was gone by the time patrol got there. Of course."

CHAPTER 6

Dani woke up and looked at the bedside clock. It was four-eighteen and pitch black outside. She'd been asleep a little less than two hours.

Bo opened his eyes and raised his head, looking at her. He stretched on his brown fleece covered dog bed and moaned loudly.

"Sorry, boy." Dani sat up and pushed herself off the bed. She rolled her head in a circle as she walked to the bathroom. Dani followed what was now becoming her morning routine. She took a quick shower, left the house with wet hair, and grabbed coffee at the convenience store. Today she added a bottle of ibuprofen to her purchase. Dani took four of them with coffee, drinking the rest on the first cup on the way to work.

As Dani sat at her office desk, the crushing responsibility for the fate of Josie and Terra hit her. Panic started to squeeze her chest. Dani took two Xanax out of her front pants pocket and washed them down with coffee. She wasn't sure whether the nausea she felt was from thinking about the two women or the lack of sleep. Dani lowered her head between her knees and took deep breaths.

"Are you alright?" Verity asked.

Dani hadn't heard him come in. She quickly sat up and said, "Just stretching my back."

"You're very pale."

Powers entered the room and said, "Well, I see that none of us could sleep." He handed Verity a sheet of paper. "Transcript of Michael's phone call to Dani last night."

Dani changed the subject. "Did you get a report from patrol on Damian Moss?"

Verity nodded. "He went straight home after the search. His mother arrived a few minutes later. Moss turned off the lights after she left at nine thirty, and never left the house."

Dani said, "So, we can eliminate Damian as a suspect. If he didn't leave his house, there's no way he could have known that Tate had come by."

Verity said, "I agree. That leaves us with Howland as our prime suspect."

"That doesn't make sense." Dani shook her head. "If Tate's the perp, he wouldn't be angry at himself for being at my place."

Verity said, "If he's smart, which he is, he could be trying to throw us off. It stands to reason that by now he knows that I've been asking about him."

Dani said, "He didn't mention it to me last night."

"Again, if he's smart, he wouldn't have."

Powers said, "Or, he might not know."

"Either way, I am going to pull patrol off Moss and put them on Howland. I am getting pressure from my boss, who is getting pressure from the governor. We must show progress."

Powers' brow furrowed. "Pressure from above? That's your reason for targeting Howland?"

Verity jutted his chin out. "I have made a decision. Why I made it is not relative."

Alyce Ryder interrupted as she hustled into the detectives' office. Dani introduced her to Verity. Alyce moved to Dani's desk and said, "I pushed a friend at the state crime lab, and he emailed me an advance copy of their report on Josie Aiken's car." She handed the report to Dani. "The only latents that could be eliminated were hers, her husband George, and her boss Dayton Cooke."

Powers said, "Who was, by the way, also her lover."

Ryder's eyes grew wide. She shook her head in dismay. "What was Josie thinking? Her husband's a hottie, and her boss most definitely is not."

Dani said, "Power and money are two huge motivators for some people." Dani held up the report. "Thanks for bringing this, Alyce. We really appreciate it."

"Sorry it's not more help." Ryder turned and left, shaking her head again.

Powers asked Verity, "Did you come up with any brilliant ideas last night on how to proceed?"

Verity said, "The problem with hard cases is that they're truly hard."

Powers rolled his eyes and said, "Wise words, indeed." Powers' cell phone rang. He looked at the caller identification. "It's dispatch."

Dani held her breath as she watched Powers listen to the voice on the other end of the call. "Got it. Ryder's in the building. Contact her and have her meet us there. We're on our way." Powers disconnected. "Patrol found Terra's car. It's at God's Word Church on Highway 93 North."

Verity said, "Looks like Michael's following the same pattern of leaving the victim's car at a church. But, he's speeding up his timeline."

Powers asked him, "You coming?"

Verity's eyes flicked to Dani. He looked back at Powers and said, "I need to follow up on some things, so I won't be joining you."

Powers said, "We'll be back before the press conference." Dani pulled her handbag out of the bottom drawer and slung it over her shoulder. The detectives rushed out to their SUV. As usual, Powers drove. They arrived at the church and saw that Terra's car was parked in a lot behind it. The patrol deputy that found the car had blocked the entrance to the parking lot with his vehicle.

Dani noted that to the east of the lot was a child care facility and to the south was an apartment complex. "It's going to take some time to interview everyone in those apartments."

"I'll call Tirrell and see if we can get a couple of patrol deputies here to help."

The rest of the crime scene team arrived before Powers had finished his phone call. They all gathered their equipment and assembled by Terra's car.

Powers said, "You all know what to do. Divide it up and get it done."

At eight forty-five, Powers and Dani left the rest of the team to finish processing the car. Two patrol deputies were busy interviewing residents of the apartment complex.

Powers pulled up to the Justice Center five minutes before the press conference was to begin. A podium had been set up outside the front doors. Reporters were busy affixing recording devices and microphones to it.

Dani could see that all the major broadcasters were represented. She said, "I'm going in the side door."

"Good idea." Powers drove around to the side entrance and parked in front of the door. When Dani looked questioningly at him, he said, "I'll move it after the press has left."

When the detectives reached their office, Tirrell and Verity were standing in the doorway waiting for them. The sheriff said, "Let's go get this dang thing over with."

Verity said, "Of course there will be no mention to the press of the notes or phone calls to Detective McKenna."

Powers mumbled, "Duh."

The four walked down the hallway and out of the front doors. Tirrell stepped up to the podium. Powers and Verity moved to stand behind him, one on each side. Dani stood next to Powers, then shifted until she was a little behind him. She would have preferred to not be there at all.

Tirrell introduced himself, then said, "The Flathead County Sheriff's Department is working with the FBI to solve a murder that occurred this past Wednesday morning. The victim has been identified as thirty-year-old Josie Aiken from Kalispell. Her body has been sent to the Montana State Crime Lab in Missoula for an autopsy to pinpoint the cause of death. We will not be answering any questions on this ongoing investigation."

A reporter in the crowd yelled, "Aw, come on, sheriff. Give us a break."

Tirrell remained stone-faced. "Thank you all for coming today."

The four quickly walked back inside the Center. The press followed them, shouting questions. A uniformed patrol deputy stepped in front of the doors, blocking access. The look on his face put an end to any further attempt to enter the building.

Powers and Dani had just sat at their desks when Connie shuffled in and said, "Terra's cell phone provider called. Her phone's back on." She handed a slip of paper to Verity. "It's at this location."

Powers rubbed his hair. "I guess we know what that means. I'll call dispatch and get Alyce, Nash, and Mercer there."

Verity jotted down the coordinates and held them out to Powers. Verity said, "I'll be right behind you. While your team processes the site, I'll talk to the people that live nearby. Richards and Webb, while we do that, I want you to interview Terra's neighbors."

As the detectives were walking to their SUV, Powers called dispatch from his cell phone. Inside the vehicle, Powers handed Dani the piece of paper with the location of Terra's cell phone on it.

Dani entered the coordinates into the GPS. She said, "This is on Valley Drive." Dani quoted part of the first note from Michael. "In your valleys shall they fall that are slain with the sword."

Valley Drive was relatively close to the Justice Center, so it only took the detectives ten minutes to get there. When they were close to the coordinates, Powers pulled off of the asphalt road and onto the shoulder. The GPS showed that the location of Terra's phone was to their right.

Dani looked across the grassy field toward the five large pine trees that stood in the middle. "If Michael's following the same pattern as with Josie, we'll find Terra's body by those trees."

Dani and Powers got out of the vehicle and walked through the tall grass. Dani didn't hurry, dreading what they would find. She realized that Powers was also moving slower than usual.

When the two detectives arrived at the trees, they saw that Terra's naked body was tied to the pine tree that was farthest from the road. Like Josie, she'd been posed with her arms behind her and her legs spread. Terra's breasts and genitals had been completely removed. Her torso was almost entirely covered with blood. Terra's cell phone was sticking out of her slack mouth.

Verity walked up behind the detectives. "Lust murders usually evolve over time and become increasingly violent. Michael's escalating."

Dani reached into her pants pocket and removed a Xanax pill. She turned her head away and dry swallowed it.

Powers said, "Not much blood on the ground. She was killed somewhere else. Like Josie."

The rest of the crime scene team arrived within fifteen minutes. The team began processing Terra's body and the surrounding area. Verity started at the north end of Valley Drive, interviewing the people that lived in the houses along it.

Before the team had finished processing the site, Powers' cell phone rang. After disconnecting, he told Dani, "We have a witness. At the daycare where Terra's car was left."

Dani said, "Maybe we'll finally get a break."

"Take the SUV and go talk to her," Powers said. "Keys are in it."

Dani nodded. She removed her protective coveralls, gloves, and booties and gave them to Ryder. Dani's heart felt heavy as she walked back to the vehicle. She hadn't been able to prevent another innocent young woman from being murdered.

Dylan Doherty, the youngest patrol deputy at the sheriff's department, was waiting for Dani at the front door of Summit Day Care. Doherty's baby face showed excitement.

Dani walked up to him and asked, "What do you have?"

Doherty motioned for Dani to follow him inside. A petite young woman with short, pink-tipped, blonde hair was bent at the waist. She was cleaning a small table with six little chairs surrounding it. She looked up and smiled at Doherty. The woman had a button nose, rosebud lips, and big green eyes. Dani thought her elfin look fit in perfectly with the surroundings.

Doherty smiled back at the woman as she walked over to them. He introduced Dani, then said, "Detective, this is Holly

Barton. Holly, please tell Detective McKenna what you told me earlier."

Holly nodded. "I got here about five thirty. I wanted to get everything done before the Farmer's Market opened at seven. A few minutes after I got here, a car pulled into the parking lot behind the church. Its headlights flashed in the front windows as it pulled in. That's how I knew it was there. Since I was here alone, I got a little nervous. So, I turned off the lights and peeked out the window. After the man parked the car, he turned off the headlights and got out. Then, he just walked away." Holly pointed. "He cut across the parking lot towards Burns Way."

Dani asked, "Could you see what he looked like?"

Holly said, "Yes. It was dark outside, but I got a good look at him when he opened the car door. The light inside came on. He had dark brown hair with a side part. It was neat, like Dylan's." Holly smiled at Doherty again.

"Was he short or tall? Heavy or thin?" Dani asked.

"He was definitely taller than average. Maybe six one or so. And, he didn't look heavy. He wasn't skinny either. I guess he would be called medium build."

Holly looked so innocent that Dani hated to introduce her to the ugliness of humanity. "I need you to come with me to the Justice Center so that we can develop a composite sketch of the man you saw. When we're finished, a patrol deputy will drive you back here."

Holly asked, "Does this have anything to do with that woman that was murdered? I saw the sheriff on TV."

Dani said, "Sorry. We can't discuss any ongoing cases."

"I understand," Holly said. "I'll get my purse."

As Dani was driving Holly to the Center, she explained the process. When they arrived, the two women went directly to Dani's office. Dani sat at her desk and pulled a chair over for Holly. "Have a seat."

Holly sat down and nervously wiped her hands on the front of her jeans.

Dani said, "Let's start with the shape of his face."

"It was oval."

Dani pulled up men's oval faces on her computer. "Which shape best resembles the man's?"

Holly pointed to one with a slightly square chin.

"Good. What color was the man's skin?"

"Regular tan? Not light or dark."

Dani tapped a few keys, and the face on the screen was filled in with color. "You said his hair was dark brown with a side part?"

Holly nodded. "Yes."

Dani hit a few keys and hair appeared on top of the face. "How's that?"

"It was a little shorter on the sides."

"Okay." Dani tapped keys.

"That's better," Holly said.

"Were his eyebrows the same color as his hair?"

"I believe so."

"Look at these and pick out the shape and thickness of his eyebrows."

Holly studied the screen, then pointed. "These ones."

"What about the color of his eyes?"

"I'm not sure what color they were, Holly said. "I got the impression that they were dark. But that could be wrong."

"We'll go with brown. It's the most common color of eyes."

Dani and Holly continued with the man's nose, mouth, lips, and ears. A little over two hours later, they'd finished a facial sketch that looked like the man Holly had seen.

Dani handed Holly a business card. "If you think of anything else, please give me a call." Dani led Holly to Connie's desk. "Connie, will you see if Dylan Doherty's available to drive Holly home?"

Holly smiled shyly at Dani and blushed. "Thanks."

Dani thanked Holly and took the sketch to Tirrell. "We have a witness who saw the man that abandoned Terra's car." Dani handed the sheriff the printed copy. "It's very close to the sketch that kid, Bryant Willis, worked up."

Tirrell studied it and handed it back. "Finally. A break."

Verity came into Tirrell's office. He looked like he might actually smile for the first time. "Around nine thirty this morning, a woman that lives on Valley Drive saw a man driving a white, two-door, Ford F-150. The man had on a blue hoody and turned his head away as they passed on the road. She didn't see what he looked like, but she was sure about the truck because her husband drives one."

Tirrell said, "Unfortunately, so do the majority of people in Montana."

Dani said, "But, we also have a better composite sketch now." She handed Verity the picture and filled him in on what Holly has seen.

Tirrell said, "I just got back from telling Terra's fiancé, Elliot Grey, that we found her body. Terra's parents live in Billings. Grey wanted to be the one to inform them of her death. I told him it's a tuff thing to do, but he insisted."

Verity said, "We need to get in front of the press on this."

Tirrell asked, "Are you suggesting another press conference?"

Verity nodded. "Yes. With the sketch and truck information, we can ask for the public's help identifying Michael."

Dani said, "We'll be inundated with calls from every crack-pot in the country."

Tirrell said, "I'll bring Detectives Tipton and Martell in full-time and put them on the phones. They can follow up with any actual leads." Tirrell yelled at his office door, "Connie!"

The secretary came around the corner.

Tirrell said, "Set up a press conference for nine in the morning."

"Am I givin' them a subject?" Connie asked.

153

"No."

Connie nodded. "I'll get right on it."

As soon as the secretary had disappeared around the corner, Dani could hear her making phone calls.

Verity said, "Sheriff, you can introduce me, then I'll take it from there."

Tirrell's head bobbed in agreement. "My pleasure."

Dani said, "I'll take both the sketch and vehicle description to dispatch so that we can get patrol on the lookout." Dani went back to her office, printed four copies of the sketch, and put one on each desk. Then, she took a copy down the hall to dispatch.

When Dani returned to the detectives' office, she saw that Webb and Richards were back. They reported to Verity that none of Terra's neighbors had seen anything helpful. Verity told the agents about finding Terra's body and filled them in on the two witnesses.

Dani pointed. "I put a copy of the new sketch on your desks."

Webb studied the picture of Michael. "We need to find this monster before he kills someone else."

Verity held up some papers and said, "The state crime lab couriered over the preliminary report on Josie Aiken's body."

154

Dani, Richards, and Webb were all staring at Verity, so he read out loud. "Victim had seventeen stab wounds to her chest, abdomen, and groin. The victim didn't have any defensive wounds. She'd been sexually assaulted more than once." Verity cleared his throat, then continued reading. "Trace evidence collected contained unidentified fibers. Dirt and debris matched the area where the body was left. No DNA or fingerprints were present. The victim had abrasions on her wrists and ankles where they had been bound by a one inch wide metal object. Light abrasions from where she was tied to the tree post-mortem. Toxicology findings showed trace amounts of ketamine in the victim's system."

Dani said, "Michael probably drugged Josie when he first kidnapped her. If he left her in his vehicle like we suspect, he would have wanted her to be unconscious so she couldn't make any noise."

Verity nodded. "That would explain why there were only trace amounts of the drug left." Verity read from the last page. "Perp was between six feet and six feet two inches in height and was right handed. Weight was between one hundred and eighty and two hundred pounds."

Dani said, "That fits with the video of the guy here at the Center and both witnesses."

Verity read the final conclusions. "Cause of death was organ failure as a result of the wounds. Time of death was between two and five Wednesday morning."

Dani spent the rest of the evening looking for speeding and parking tickets over the past week for a white F-150 pickup. There were seven speeding tickets and two parking tickets. She checked the location of each of them. None were issued near the Justice Center, or the site of the abandoned cars and bodies.

Powers came back to the office around nine that night. The three FBI agents had already left. Powers rubbed his hand over his hair. "Get your stuff. I'm going to follow you home. I want to be there when Michael calls."

"Why?"

Powers said, "Because this guy's escalating and I don't want you to be alone when he calls tonight." Dani started to speak, but Powers interrupted. "Don't argue. I'm too tired to get into it with you."

Dani nodded. "Okay."

"Before we get to your house, pull over somewhere that I can leave my truck. I'll ride with you from there. I don't want Michael to know I'm with you."

156

Fifteen minutes later, Dani pulled off and waited for Powers to get in. They didn't speak until Dani had parked in her garage. She pushed the button on the remote to close the garage door behind them. After it was completely down, Dani said, "We're clear."

Powers sat up from where he'd been lying on the back seat of Dani's Jeep. He opened the door and let himself out.

Dani locked the Jeep and led Powers inside the house. Bo was waiting at the door with his legs spread in a fighting stance. He growled and barked at Powers. Dani told Bo it was okay. She rubbed his ears for a couple of seconds before moving into the kitchen.

"Wow!" Powers said, looking around the great-room. He walked over to the large front windows and took in the view. "This place is fantastic."

"Thanks. I like it."

Powers turned to Dani. "The least you could have done was invite me over for a beer. You know I live in that dinky apartment with one window that looks at the parking lot."

Dani said, "I'd offer you a beer, but the only thing I have to drink is Chardonnay."

Powers grinned. "In that case, Chardonnay sounds perfect."

Dani poured wine into two glasses, holding one out to Powers.

"Thanks," he said, taking the glass.

Dani carried the wine to the living room and sat on the couch. "Have a seat."

Powers followed, sitting in one of the armchairs. He sipped from his glass and sighed. "I'm beat. How are you doing? This must be ten times worse for you."

Dani shrugged. "I'm not having fun. But I'm sure Josie's and Terra's families are doing worse than I am." Dani sighed. "I really want to put Michael behind bars."

"Me too. But, first I'd like to get a few minutes alone with him."

Dani visibly shivered. "Not me. I want as far away from that guy as possible." Dani gulped a mouthful of wine.

The sat in silence for a few seconds, then Powers asked, "Is there any particular reason why you don't trust people?"

Dani didn't immediately respond. Finally, she said, "I've found that, in general, people aren't trustworthy." She drained her glass and rose from the couch. "I'm getting a refill. Do you want one?"

"I'm good," Powers said, holding up his half-full glass.

Dani went to the kitchen and poured herself more wine. As she was walking back to the couch, her cell phone rang. Dani looked at the caller identification. "Unknown. It's him." Dani put her cell phone on the coffee table, swiped the answer icon, and put the phone on speaker. "Detective McKenna."

"So formal tonight. Is that because your boss is there?"

Powers stood, strolled over to the room's picture window, and looked out across the lake.

Michael asked, "Why are you so quiet, Dani?"

Powers turned around and motioned with his finger for Dani to keep talking. He hid his hand in front of his body so that anyone looking from the outside wouldn't be able to see it.

Dani asked, "Why are you calling, Michael?"

"To talk to you, of course."

Powers walked back over to the coffee table and said, "Hey, Dani. Where's the restroom?" He moved toward the door that Dani had pointed at. Once inside the guest bathroom, Powers closed the door and quickly called dispatch. "Get all available units over to Island Drive, immediately!" Powers explained that the murderer was there and watching Dani's house.

Michael asked, "Do you have me on speaker phone?"

"Detective Powers went to the restroom. He can't hear us."

Michael was silent for a second before saying, "I want to have time alone with you. For these brief moments, I want you all to myself."

"If that's true, why don't you come get me? We could be alone together."

Powers came back into the room in time to hear what Dani had said. He scowled at her.

Dani ignored him. "How does that sound, Michael?"

"Not yet. I'm not ready."

Dani said, "Why take other women?"

"I'll explain when we see each other again. I love you. Good night." Michael ended the call.

Dani picked up her cell phone and hurled it across the room. The fractured pieces made a tinkling sound as they slid across the hard tile floor.

Powers raised one eyebrow. He sat back in the armchair and sipped from his glass.

Dani drank all of the wine in her glass. She carried it to the kitchen and refilled it for a third time. She fished around in her pants pocket until she found a Xanax. Dani washed it down with wine. She blinked rapidly, but couldn't keep tears from running down her cheeks. Bo came to Dani's side and looked up at her. She dried her face with a paper towel, then leaned over and kissed the top of Bo's head. "You're the only good thing in my life."

Powers picked up the remote control for the television and turned it on. He scrolled through the listings and selected 'The Notebook'. Powers shifted in the chair and sipped Chardonnay.

"What are you doing?" Dani asked as she poured more wine into her glass.

"Settling in."

"Why?"

"You're sure as hell not driving me back to my truck tonight. And, I'm too tired to walk. So, you're stuck with me for the night. What do you have to eat?"

"Peanut butter."

Powers turned up the volume on the television and went into the kitchen. "Go sit on the couch and watch the movie. It's great."

Dani wobbled a little as she made her way to the couch. She flopped down, sloshing wine on the front of her shirt. Bo sat on the rug next to the couch and put his head on Dani's knee. She rubbed his snout. "What's this movie?" Dani asked.

Powers incredulously said, "You've never seen this? It's a classic love story."

"That would be why I've never watched it."

Powers buttered the toast he'd made. Then, he slathered on peanut butter and strawberry jelly. "You don't believe in love?"

"No."

Powers opened cabinet doors until he found what he was looking for. Taking two saucers out, he set them on the countertop. Powers put a piece of toast on each one. He carried them to the living room and handed one to Dani. He sat in the armchair and ate while watching the movie.

Dani mindlessly ate all of her toast. "That was good. Thanks." She set the saucer on the coffee table and stretched out on the couch. Dani fell asleep almost immediately.

Bo began growling. He ran to the front door and barked at something outside. Dani slept through the noise. Powers stood and drew his handgun. He moved to the front door and looked out the peephole. Tate Howland was standing on the porch.

Powers holstered his gun and took out his cell phone. He found Howland in his contacts and pressed the call icon. Powers watched as Howland removed his phone from inside his suit jacket, swiped the screen, and held it to his ear. When Howland answered, Powers said, "I'm inside. Dani's dead to the world, and I don't know the security code to open the door."

"No problem. I came by to check on her." He paused. "She might try to hide it, but this case has been hard on her."

"I'm aware."

Howland nodded. "Well, I'm glad you're with her. I'll see you at the Center."

Powers disconnected. Bo trotted back to Dani's side and stood watching Powers. He held up both hands and said, "Good boy. Stay. Stay." Powers slowly walked into Dani's bedroom. Picking up the bottle of Xanax that was sitting on the nightstand, he read the label.

CHAPTER 7

Dani became aware of an intense pain in her head. She opened her eyes and silently cursed herself. Turning her head, she saw that Powers was slumped sideways, asleep in the chair. Bo was sitting on his haunches watching Powers. Dani gave Bo a hug around the neck. She sat up and rubbed her forehead. A large glass of water and two ibuprofen were sitting on the coffee table. Dani downed both.

Powers stirred, then sat up. He looked at Dani. "How's your head?"

"It's been better. Give me ten minutes to shower, then I'll drop you off at your truck." Dani closed the bedroom door after Bo was inside. She undressed, dropping her clothes on the floor of the bathroom. Dani turned the shower on, letting the warm water wrap her in a cocoon. She would have liked to stay there, isolated from the outside world. Dani dressed in clean clothes, moving her gun holster and cell phone holder to the new pair of pants.

When Dani emerged from the bedroom, Powers pushed himself out of the chair. He stretched his arms over his head and groaned. "Boy, do I need a shower and coffee."

164

Dani said, "Thanks for coming over last night. I was glad you were here when Michael starts."

Powers shrugged. "That's what partners and friends do."

Dani patted the empty cell phone carrying case on her side. "I'm going to need a new phone. The last one suddenly stopped working."

With a straight face, Powers said, "I hate when that happens."

Dani chuckled. "Come on. Let's go." She drove Powers to his truck. When he stepped out, she said, "Thanks again." Powers patted the top of the Jeep and closed the door.

On the way to the Justice Center, Dani stopped at the convenience store and bought two large coffees. She took a drink out of one disposable cup, burning the top of her mouth with the hot liquid. Dani blew through the slit in the top of the cup. She continued to blow and sip as she drove to the Justice Center. As Dani walked into the lobby, she saw Tate Howland coming down the stairs.

Tate said, "Good morning."

"Not really."

Tate frowned. "Bad night?"

"Bad week." Dani didn't stop to chat. She kept walking to her office. In the room, Dani saw that Verity was already there, sitting at his table.

Verity said, "I hear Michael was watching you and Powers last night. Perhaps today's search of Island Drive will yield something."

Dani hoped her face didn't give away the fact that she didn't know there was a search happening. "If we're lucky."

When Powers walked into the office twenty minutes later, he said, "Search of the east shore of the peninsula hasn't yielded anything useful yet. Patrol deputies will also go door-to-door to see if the residents have noticed an unknown man hanging around."

Verity said, "It's possible he wasn't on the peninsula. He could have followed you from here."

Powers shook his head. "I was watching. If anyone had been following us, I would have seen them. Bo would have let us know if someone was close to the house. The only other place with a clear view into Dani's living room is from across the lake."

"I see." Verity looked at Dani. "Any new thoughts on why Michael is contacting you? Or what this connection is that he talked about?"

Dani shook her head. "None."

Verity leaned back in his chair. "I know you're not telling the truth."

Powers glared. "The truth is that you don't know shit."

Verity said to Dani, "I'm going to find out what you're lying about."

Powers jumped up from his chair, fists balled. Dani stood and moved to Powers. "Ignore him. That's what I'm going to do." She walked out of the office and down the hall to the bathroom. Dani took a Xanax pill out of her pants pocket, swallowed it with water from the sink, and squeezed her eyes shut. She took several deep breaths, trying to quiet her beating heart.

Powers pushed the bathroom door open and came inside.

Dani spun around. "What are you doing?" Dani said, "This is the women's restroom."

Powers ran his hand back and forth over his bristly hair. "You have a problem with those pills you're taking?" He put his back against the door, preventing anyone else from entering. "I know about them."

"They're prescribed by my doctor. I don't have a problem with them."

167

"I know this case has been tough on you. You don't eat. You're drinking more than usual. And, now you're taking anti-anxiety meds. I'm concerned."

Dani rubbed her forehead. "I'm okay... really."

Powers sighed. "If you're ever not okay, I hope you know you can talk to me." Powers patted Dani on the shoulder, then turned and left.

Dani took a deep breath and said out loud to herself, "Come on. Get it together."

Verity's eyes watched Dani as she came back into the room, but he didn't say anything.

Powers cell rang. He looked at the caller identification. "It's Ryder. She's with Paget, Nash, and Mercer on the search." Powers answered, listened, then said, "Thanks for letting me know. See you back here." Powers disconnected and said, "The only thing they found were some tracks on the beach. Men's size twelve. Ryder took a mold of it." Powers shrugged. "Of course we can't be sure that it's from Michael."

Verity asked, "What about the residents? Did they see anyone out of place?"

Powers shook his head. "No."

An alarm on Verity's cell phone started beeping. He stood. "It's time to gather for the press conference. Dani walked with Powers and Verity to the lobby. Tirrell was standing at the front doors, watching through the glass as different stations attached their microphones to the podium. Emmerson Wilson had made all the arrangements for Michael's sketch to be displayed on-air.

Verity turned to Dani. "I'd like you to sit this one out. Michael wants to see you on TV, so we're not going to give him what he wants. Let him know he's not pulling all the strings."

Dani nodded. "I'm good with that."

At nine o'clock sharp, Tirrell, Verity, and Powers stepped up to the podium. Tirrell said, "A second young woman's body was discovered yesterday morning. The victim has been identified as Miss Terra Tucker. The Federal Bureau of Investigation has taken the lead in this case." Tirrell stepped back and nodded to Verity.

Verity took Tirrell's place in the middle of the podium. He held up his hand to silence the questions that were being hurled at him. "I am FBI Assistant Special Agent in Charge, Hal Verity. A witness has provided us with this composite sketch of the suspect." The sketch appeared in the upper right corner of viewers' television screens. The number of the tip line appeared in the left corner. "We believe the suspect is approximately six foot two feet tall and weighs one hundred and ninety pounds.

He's driving a two-door, white, Ford F-150 truck. If anyone has any information regarding this man, please call the number on your screen."

A reporter shouted, "Are you saying the same man killed both women?"

Verity shook his head. "At this early stage in the investigation, we cannot say that with certainty."

The same reporter shouted, "But there could be a serial killer walking around town?!"

"As I said, it is too early in the investigation to draw any conclusions." Verity held up his hand for silence. "Again, we urge the public to call the tip line if they have any information. Thank you." Verity walked away, with Tirrell and Powers on his heels.

Dani turned and moved back into the lobby, almost running into Tate. He asked, "Everything go okay with the press conference?"

"Verity doesn't want to give Michael the pleasure of seeing me on TV. So, I just watched."

Powers stopped and thumped Tate on the back. "How's it going?"

"Good. You?"

"Peachy."

Dani glanced out the front doors at the dispersing press. A man standing on the sidewalk caught her eye. She could see that from under the brim of his navy baseball cap he was looking in at her. Powers had his back to the doors. Dani said to him, "Don't turn around. There's a man in a baseball hat outside watching me."

Powers nodded and said, "I'll go out the side door." He turned and casually walked down the corridor. When Powers reached the door, he drew his gun, peeked around the corner of the building, and rushed forward.

The man saw Powers. He turned and started running across the parking lot. Dani sprinted across the lobby. She stiff armed one of the doors open with so much force that it slammed back against the wall. Dani ran, following the man across the parking lot.

Powers was already in pursuit. He shoved his gun back into its holster and pointed for Dani to go left. Powers veered right.

Dani yelled, "Police! Stop!"

The man didn't break stride or look behind him. He ran out of the parking lot, across the street, and into a thick hedge of

Cypress. Powers sprinted down the sidewalk, heading to the north end of the trees.

Dani lost sight of the man, but she followed him into the hedge. She ducked her head and pushed her way between two trees. Suddenly, Dani was tackled from behind. Her chest slammed onto the leaf covered ground, forcing the air in her lungs out. The years of training kicked in automatically. She flipped sideways breaking the man's hold on her and stood up. As the man was getting to his feet, Dani punched him in the temple. He emitted a loud grunt and swung blindly at Dani. She blocked his shot with her left arm as she slugged him in the neck with her right fist. The man coughed. He quickly threw another punch at Dani, catching her on the side of her nose and cheek. She staggered backward, giving the man an opportunity to sprint away. Blood began running out of Dani's nose, but she ignored it. She followed after the man, emerging from the trees to see Powers standing a few yards away. Dani held up both hands. "Where did he go?!"

Powers shook his head. "I didn't see him." He called dispatch on his cell and told them to have patrol cars search the area. He strode over to Dani. Powers' eyes grew wide when he saw the blood from her nose. "Are you okay?"

Dani tilted her head back. "It was Michael. I recognized him from the sketches." Dani unbuttoned the cuff of her shirt sleeve and used it to pinch her nostrils closed, curtailing most of the bleeding.

Powers said, "Come on. Let's get you to the Center and take a look at that nose."

Dani breathed through her mouth as she and Powers made their way back. Powers was winded. He noisily dragged air into his lungs as they walked. Under his arms, big circles of sweat stained his shirt.

Tate stood on the front sidewalk, watching the detectives approach. Seeing the blood on Dani's shirt, he rushed to her. "Are you alright?"

Dani took the cuff of her shirt away from her nose. "I'm fine. It's not broken."

Tate asked, "How do you know?"

"My nose has been broken before."

Powers said, "This is when I'd normally make a comment about you needlessly getting yourself injured in those sparring sessions of yours. But I'm not going to say anything because without them Michael would probably have hurt you a lot worse."

"I got one good jab in. Michael's going to have a black eye."

"Glad to hear it," Tate said. "That SOB deserves much worse." Back inside the lobby of the Center, he said, "I've got an ice pack in my office. Hang on a sec, and I'll go get it." Tate took the stairs three at a time. When he returned and handed the ice pack to Dani, she thanked him.

As the detectives were walking toward their office, Dani detoured into the women's restroom. She cupped her hands under the sink's running water and washed the blood off of her face. Dani removed her shirt and let cold water run over the sleeve and front until the red had faded to pink. She shivered when she put the shirt back on.

When Dani walked into her office, she saw that another folding table had been brought in. Detectives Tipton and Martell were sitting side by side at the table. They both had a phone pressed to their ear, and were taking notes as they listened.

Verity said, "It's a shame that you let Michael get away."

From his desk, Powers said, "How did you become such an ass?"

Dani sat on her chair and placed the ice pack on her nose. She asked Verity, "What do you make of Michael showing up at the press conference? Seems like he was taking quite a chance."

Verity said, "He was taunting us. Showing us that he's smarter than us."

174

Powers asked, "I'd like to know how he found out about it."

Verity shrugged. "There are any number of ways. He could have overheard someone talking about it. Or, he might know someone who works for the press."

When Powers cell phone rang, he answered and listened to the voice on the other end. Finally, he said, "Appreciate the call." Powers disconnected. "No sign of Michael or his Ford anywhere near the Center."

Dani said, "I'm sure he had the truck parked close by. Got in it and took off before patrol arrived."

Verity said, "If only Detective McKenna hadn't let Michael escape, we'd have him right now."

Powers narrowed his eyes at Verity and said, "Shut your mouth, asshole."

The other agents and detectives in the room stopped and stared. Martell asked, "Hey, anyone want to hear a joke?"

Verity said, "No."

Martell said, "Great! What kind of mushroom likes to party? A fungi." When nobody smiled, he said, "Here's another one. What did the ghost say to the wall? Just passing through." Martell looked around the room. "Okay, last one. Who can shave twenty-five times a day and still have a beard? A barber."

Powers shook his head. "None of those are even slightly funny."

Martell frowned. "That hurts my feelings."

Dani looked at Martell and mouthed "Thanks."

Verity insisted on immediately taking a statement from Dani and Powers about their encounter with Michael.

As Powers talked, Dani studied Josie's autopsy report, which had arrived earlier. Verity had read it, but she hoped there might be something he'd missed. It was a futile hope.

Shortly after Dani had relayed the details of her altercation with Michael, Connie delivered the lab results on the third note. She gave Dani a mournful look, then turned around and left the office.

Verity read the report. He shook his head. "No evidence of any kind."

Powers said, "Of course not."

At five o'clock the phone line for reporting information about Michael was transferred to a message machine. Everyone in the office was tired and agreed that they should head home. If

Michael followed the pattern, Dani would receive another note tomorrow.

Dani felt bone weary as she drove home. Even though the trip only took fifteen minutes, she felt like it lasted a full hour. When Dani arrived, she hugged Bo, filled his water bowl, and poured herself a glass of wine. Dani took the wine to the bathroom and ran a hot bath for herself. She poured lavender scented bath salts into the tub and stripped. As she lowered herself into the warm water, she sighed. Dani sipped wine, trying to keep her mind from roaming into dark places.

Dani jumped when Bo began growling. A second later, the doorbell rang and Bo started barking loudly. Dani bolted out of the bathtub. Every muscle in her body was tense and her nerves were humming. She dried herself off and slipped on a blue terry robe. Dani picked up her Glock from the nightstand in her bedroom and carried it to the front door. Bo continued barking as he walked alongside her. She looked out the peephole and saw Tate Howland standing in front of the door. Dani was caught off guard when she realized that she was glad to see him. She disarmed the security system, unlocked the door, pulled it open, and invited Tate inside.

Tate smiled widely, causing his dimples to appear. He stepped inside and held up a large bag, saying, "Sandwiches, chips, and chocolate chip cookies."

Dani smiled. "I didn't realize until just now that I'm starving." She locked the door and armed the security system. Turning to Tate, she said, "I'll get plates and wine." Dani placed her gun on the island and moved around to the refrigerator. She topped off her glass of Chardonnay and poured one for Tate. Dani put the plates and napkins on the island.

Bo ran back to the front door and began barking again. Dani walked back around the island, picking up her Glock as she passed it. She looked out the peep hole and saw Todd Nash standing on the porch. Dani disarmed the alarm, unlocked the door, and opened it.

Nash didn't wait to be invited. He stepped inside, looked at Tate, and asked Dani, "You okay?"

Dani nodded. "I'm fine. Really."

Nash said, "I tried calling, but there was no answer."

Dani patted the pockets of her robe. "I left my phone next to the bathtub. Sorry."

"No problem."

Looking at Dani, Tate said, "I'm glad the department has assigned someone to watch you."

Dani was too tired to pretend. "They haven't. They're actually following you."

"Me? Why?"

"Because Verity thinks you could be the bible quoting murderer."

There was complete silence for at least ten seconds. Then, Tate said, "Todd, do you want to join us for dinner? There's plenty."

Nash shook his head. "Mercer's actually taking over for me in a few minutes, so I'll wait for him outside."

Dani locked the door behind Nash and rearmed the security system. She patted Bo, who had clearly been uncomfortable with that many strangers in the house. "I'll be right back," Dani said. "I'm going to put some clothes on." She dressed in warm-ups, an oversized sweatshirt, and thick socks.

When Dani returned to the kitchen, she found Tate loading the plates with thick turkey sandwiches. Dani carried the wine glasses to the dining room table, and Tate took their plates.

The two ate in silence until Tate asked, "So, do you think I'm the murderer?"

"No." Dani shook her head, then started eating again.

When they had both finished, Tate cleared the table and loaded the dishes into the dishwasher. While he was doing that, Dani refilled their glasses and took them to the living room. She sat on one end of the couch and pulled her legs under her.

Tate sat in the corner on the opposite side of the couch. He leaned back, stretched his long legs out in front, and looked at Dani. "How's your nose?"

Dani probed the bridge and sides of her nose. "It's sore. But not too painful."

Tate sipped his wine. "I'm glad you don't think I'm the killer."

"Verity wouldn't listen to anything I said." Dani shrugged. "I guess he thinks I'm biased."

One corner of Tate's mouth turned up. "I hope you are."

"You hope I'm what?"

"Biased towards me."

Dani blushed. She looked down into her glass, then drank some wine.

Tate said, "So, tell me about yourself."

Dani involuntarily stiffened, causing Bo to turn his head toward her. Dani patted Bo and said, "There's not much to tell."

Tate sat up straighter. "There's a lot I don't know about you and would like to know."

Dani shrugged. "Like what?"

"Like, why you came here to live with your grandmother."

Dani drained her wine and walked back to the kitchen to refill it. She could feel Tate's dark eyes following her. Dani moved back to the couch and slowly sat down. She twirled her glass by the stem and said, "I had a major falling out with my mother and stepfather." She looked down into the wine. "My grandmother said I could come live with her, so I did."

"What about your birth father? Why didn't you go live with him?"

"He died when I was eleven."

Tate leaned forward and turned toward Dani. "I'm so sorry. That must have been hard."

Dani's eyes welled with tears. She blinked rapidly.

"How did he die?"

Dani drank more wine. "He killed himself," she whispered.

Tate set his wine glass on the coffee table and scooted next to Dani. He put his arms around her and pulled her toward him.

Dani's heart hammered, but she didn't pull away. She laid her cheek on Tate's chest.

Tate kissed the top of Dani's head. He softly said, "Tell me."

"I found him when I got home from school. He was in his office. He'd shot himself in the head. That was the first time I smelled cordite."

Tate pulled her closer and held on tighter.

Dani said, "Dad didn't leave a note explaining why he killed himself. But we found out later that he'd taken out a second mortgage on our home, and had invested it all in some get-rich-quick scam. My mom was a basket case. She'd never worked, and all we had left was the little bit of money that was in the bank. The first month or so she never got out of bed. The only thing she ate was what I made for her. We switched roles. I took care of her."

"I'm sorry you had to go through that."

"I think that's why she started dating my stepfather. He had money, and she was terrified of not having any. She was beautiful, educated, and subservient. She made great arm candy. It was a marriage made in heaven. Except my stepfather was

182

never thrilled that I was part of the package. Thankfully, my stepbrother was kind to me or living there would have been so much worse."

Dani sat up and pulled out of Tate's embrace. She drank the remaining wine in her glass. "I'm going to have more. Would you like some?"

"You sit. I'll fill our glasses up."

Dani watched Tate's retreating form. When she realized that she was staring, she quickly flicked her eyes away. Tate came back and handed Dani her glass. He sat beside her.

Dani said, "I've never told anyone that. I'm sorry to be such a downer."

Tate took her hand in his. "Don't be sorry. I'm not. I want to get to know you. All of you. The good and the bad."

Dani looked into Tate's eyes as he leaned toward her. She gasped when his lips touched hers. Dani couldn't believe that she wanted him to kiss her. Which he did. Until Bo started growling. Tate drew slightly back and turned his eyes toward Bo. Then, he sat back and started laughing.

Dani told Bo that it was okay. Then, she said, "Sorry about that. He's never seen anyone kiss me before."

"How's that possible?" Tate asked, looking Dani up and down. "Have you seen yourself?"

Dani blushed and mumbled something incomprehensible.

Tate looked at his watch. "Well, I have to get going anyway. It's late, and I know you must be tired." Tate got up from the couch.

Dani followed him. She disarmed the alarm, unlocked the front door, and opened it. Dani said, "Thanks for bringing food."

"Thanks for trusting me." Tate kissed Dani on the cheek, turned, and walked down the pathway. Before he got into his car, he turned back and waved at her.

Dani locked the door and rearmed the system. She drained the last of the bottle of wine into her glass. Dani sat back down on the couch and replayed Tate's kiss in her mind. The ringing of her cell phone brought her back to reality. Dani didn't bother looking at the caller identification. She knew it was Michael. Dani swiped the answer icon but didn't say anything.

"How's your nose, Dani?"

"Fine. How's your eye?"

"I have to admit. I was a little surprised by you today."

"Why is that? Because you only kidnap defenseless women?"

"They are not helpless creatures. They are evil women. The Bible says so."

"You're psychotic. That's the only reason you're taking these women."

"That's unkind, Dani. But, I forgive you. Because I love you very much. I'll talk to you soon."

Dani held onto the phone and paced, waiting for Powers to call. But she already knew what he was going to say. When Dani answered, Powers said, "Gone. Of course."

"Well, there's one piece of good news."

"What's that?"

"The patrol of the peninsula must be keeping Michael away because he didn't know that Tate was here tonight."

"Both of those things are great."

"What do you mean, both things?"

"The patrol's working and Howland was at your place again. Both are great."

"Oh shut up." Dani swiped the end call icon and washed down a Xanax with some wine. She carried her Glock as she walked

185

through the house, checking the security system and all of the locks on the doors and windows.

CHAPTER 8

The next morning Dani woke with a headache again. She promised herself that she wouldn't drink so much wine tonight. As Dani drove to the Justice Center, she found herself watching for a white Ford F-150 truck. Each time Dani saw one, she squinted until she could get a clear view of the driver.

When Dani walked into the office at eight, Verity was sitting on the edge of her desk. As she approached, he held up a sheet of paper. "Transcript of your conversation with Michael."

Dani reached for the handle of her desk drawer, but Verity's leg was in the way. She said, "Excuse me. I need to get in there."

Verity pushed off, standing next to Dani. "Do not antagonize Michael when he calls."

Dani put her handbag away and sat on her desk chair. "I was upset."

Stressing each word, Verity said, "Do you understand me?"

Dani's eyes shot sparks. She stood and squared off with Verity. "Don't ever disrespect me again by talking to me like I'm some misbehaving child."

Powers chose that moment to come into the room. He looked back and forth at Dani and Verity. The tension was palpable. He strode to Dani and asked, "What's going on?"

Dani said, "Agent Verity and I were just getting some things straight." She walked out of the office and down the hallway to the bathroom. Dani tapped the screen on her cell, entering the phone number that she still remembered from years ago. "This is Dani. I need to see you."

Dani walked back into the office a few minutes later. Without a word, she took her handbag from the bottom drawer and headed for the door.

Powers brow furrowed. "Are you going somewhere?"

"I have some personal business to take care of."

Outside, Dani checked the back of her Jeep before getting in. She sped to the house that had been a source of both pain and comfort for her. Dani parked in the driveway and examined the rambling building. The combination of the silver metal roof, red cedar siding, and barn-wood accents was still stunning. Dani stepped to the office entrance on the right, took a deep breath, and pushed the doorbell.

Except for the now salt and pepper hair, Doctor Barbara Ellison hadn't changed since the last time Dani had seen her. The sixty-two-year-old psychiatrist still wore loose flowing tops and long skirts in muted fall colors. When Doctor Ellison smiled, her smoky gray eyes crinkled at the corners. "Dani! It's so good to see you." Doctor Ellison opened the door wider. "Please come in." The psychiatrist closed and locked the door behind them. She sat in a peach colored armchair and indicated for Dani to sit in the one opposite her.

Dani sat on the edge of the chair, hands clasped together. Her eyes wandered around the room, not seeing what she was looking at.

"It's been a long time. What's troubling you?"

Dani met Doctor Ellison's gaze. "It's this case I'm working on."

The psychiatrist nodded. "I saw you on TV with the sheriff."

"What the sheriff didn't say is that the murderer's contacting me. He's been sending me messages at work and calling me every night."

"That must be frightening."

"The murderer's been talking about a special bond that we have."

Doctor Ellison leaned forward in her chair. "Do you think he could be the man that kidnapped you?"

Dani shook her head. "He can't be. I told you what I did." She paused. "I've started having flashbacks and panic attacks again."

"Do the people you work with think that the murderer might be connected in some way to the man that kidnapped you?"

"They don't know about the kidnapping."

"Have you shared with anyone what happened to you?"

"Only you."

"It's been two years since we stopped our sessions. Have you had a relationship since then?"

Dani shook her head.

"Have you been on a date?"

"No. And, I know what you're going to say. But I don't want to make myself vulnerable to anyone."

Doctor Ellison gave Dani a small smile. "Do you want to tell me about the messages and phone conversations?"

Dani nodded and relayed the details of the notes and calls from Michael.

"That tells me what happened. You didn't tell me how you're feeling."

"Scared that I'm going to be kidnapped and it will all happen again."

"That's understandable." The doctor placed her hand on top of Dani's hands. "But you're not the same person that you were at seventeen. You've attended the police academy. You've trained for years in hand-to-hand fighting. You carry a gun, and you know how to use it. I know that you are quite capable of protecting yourself. Now you need to believe that."

Dani was quiet for a couple of seconds. Then she said, "I know in my head that you're right. But, my body isn't following along with that knowledge."

"How have you been coping until now?"

"I have a bottle of Xanax that I've been taking."

Doctor Ellison took a prescription pad and pen off of the small side table next to her chair. She wrote on the pad, tore it off, and handed it to Dani. "Here's a new prescription. The old ones have probably lost some of their effectiveness."

Dani took the slip of paper and put it in her handbag. "Thank you," she said, standing.

Doctor Ellison led the way to the office door and opened it. "I hope you'll come back soon to talk."

"I don't know when I'll have a break from this case. I'll call when I do."

Doctor Ellison smiled. "I understand." She hugged Dani, went back inside, and closed the door.

Dani walked to her Jeep and checked inside, as was becoming her habit. She unlocked and opened the door, and set her handbag on the passenger seat. Looking up, Dani gasped. Under the windshield wiper was a manila envelope. She whipped around and drew her Glock. Dani rushed up and down the sidewalk, checking both sides of the street. She didn't see Michael anywhere.

Dani returned to her Jeep and removed an evidence bag and latex gloves from the pockets of her pants. She put the gloves on, removed the envelope from under the wiper, and placed it in the clear bag. Dani drove back to the Justice Center thinking about how she could explain where she'd been. She carried the manila envelope inside to the detectives' office.

Powers saw her and said, "Hey, Dani. Guess what. The women's clothing we found in Damian Moss' boxing studio didn't have Josie's or Terra's DNA on them. Isn't that amazing?!"

Dani held up the protected manila envelope.

Powers stood. "Where the hell did that come from?"

"When I came out of my doctor's appointment, I found it on the windshield of my Jeep."

Verity asked, "Did you open it?"

Dani shook her head. "I wanted to wait until I got back here." She placed the bagged envelope on her desk. Dani took a pair of latex gloves out of her desk drawer and put them on. She removed the manila envelope from inside the evidence bag and tore it open. As expected, inside was another note from Michael and two photographs of a woman.

The men gathered around Dani as she read aloud. "Dearest Dani, The Bible says 'If any prophet presumes to speak anything in my name that I have not authorized him to speak, or speaks in the name of other gods, that prophet must die.' Enclosed are photos of the prophet. I look forward to talking to you again soon. Love, Michael."

Powers said, "We have to find that psychopath before he murders this woman."

Dani put the note and photographs in separate evidence sheaths and made copies of each. She attached one set to a fourth whiteboard and pushed it to the front of the room, next to the others.

Powers stared at the two pictures of the woman. He rubbed his hair. "She looks familiar to me."

193

Dani said, "I've been thinking about how we might catch Michael. The first note said, 'In your hills, and in your valleys, and in all your rivers, shall they fall that are slain with the sword.' Josie's body was left near Hill Road, and Terra's was near Valley Drive. Hills and valleys. If Michael's following the same pattern, that leaves rivers.

Dani pulled up google maps on her computer, setting it on satellite view. I checked earlier, and there are four streets with the name River. River View Drive, River Glen Court, River Place, and River Road." She tapped on the keyboard and pointed at the monitor. "The first three roads are crowded with houses. On both sides of the street. River Road's the only one that has an open area with no houses. And, there are large trees along that stretch of the road."

"That's good thinking, McKenna," Powers said. "Michael will be looking for the right place to leave this woman's body. There are too many churches in town to watch all of them. But, we can sit on one road. I'll get patrol units to take shifts steaking out River Road. Starting now."

Verity said, "Michael might not show up there. He might have already looked for and decided on the location."

"You have any better ideas?" Powers asked.

"I was merely making a statement."

Powers said, "Stating the obvious."

Dani started typing on her computer's keyboard. She read aloud. "Synonyms for prophet are medium, clairvoyant, astrologer, meteorologist, forecaster."

Powers excitedly said, "Now I remember!" He pointed at the photographs. "She's the nightly weather person on TV. I don't remember what channel. But that's her."

Dani turned back to her computer and searched the local television stations. "You're right. Here she is. Her name's Cindi Bowers. She's on the local NBC station."

Verity said, "Powers, you and Dani go to her home address. I'll go to the TV station."

The three jogged out to their vehicles. Powers started the SUV and Dani called dispatch. As she waited for the requested information, Dani nervously tapped her right heel on the black rubber floor mat. She pulled a small notepad and a pen from inside her handbag and wrote down the make and model of Cindi Bowers' car. Dani entered Cindi's home address into the GPS and started tapping her foot again.

Tires squealed as Powers pulled out of the parking lot and again when he turned off of Ali Loop onto the paved driveway of Cindi's home. The single-story ranch was clad in pale gray wood siding with bright white trim. Powers parked the SUV in front of the double-car garage.

Dani's cell phone rang. She looked at the screen. "It's Verity." Dani swiped the answer icon and listened. She disconnected and said, "Cindi's not at work. They're expecting her to arrive within the next fifteen minutes."

Powers and Dani hurried up the flagstone path and rang the front doorbell. When there was no answer, Powers pounded on the door with his fist. Dani walked across the straw-like grass to the front picture window. She cupped her hands around her eyes and looked inside. Through the semi-sheer drapes, Dani could see vague images in the living room and kitchen beyond. "I see a man in there!"

Powers pounded on the door again and yelled, "Police!"

Dani continued to concentrate on the figure in the kitchen. Suddenly she said, "He's going out the back door!"

Powers drew his gun from its side holster. As he sprinted around the corner of the house, he yelled, "Call for backup!"

Dani called dispatch from her cell phone. Then, she drew her Glock and ran around the side of the house after Powers. Dani saw that he was chasing a tall man with brown hair across the backyard. Dani raced after them.

Powers yelled, "Police!" Then, he stopped running and took a shooting stance. Powers fired at the man. The man grabbed his left shoulder, then whirled around. He pointed the gun that he held in his right hand and shot twice at Powers. Powers dropped to the ground.

Dani screamed, "No!" As she continued running, Dani raised her Glock and fired at the man's back. He jumped over the cedar fence, ran into the trees beyond, and disappeared. Dani shoved her Glock back in its holster and dropped down next to Powers. He'd been hit in the right side. Dani called for an ambulance. She took off her jacket, wadded it up, and placed it over Powers' wound.

Powers winced when Dani pressed down. "Ease up, will you."

"The ambulance is on the way."

"I heard. I'm shot, not deaf." Powers coughed.

"Shut up, you big idiot." Dani continued to press on the wound with both hands. When she saw Verity running toward her, Dani pointed at the house. "I've got Powers. Michael was inside. Check on Cindi."

Verity nodded and sprinted to the open back door of the house.

A few minutes later, Dani heard the piercing wail of the ambulance as it arrived. The paramedics rushed to Powers, checked his vital signs, and replaced Dani's bloody jacket with a thick bandage. When they loaded Powers onto the collapsible gurney, Dani said, "I'm coming with him."

Powers shook his head. "No, you're not." He coughed. "Get the crime scene team here to process the house, and get all available patrol officers here to search those woods."

Dani walked alongside the gurney as Powers was wheeled to the ambulance. "Don't worry. You trained me. I know what to do. Concentrate on getting better."

Powers nodded and closed his eyes as the paramedics loaded him into the ambulance.

Verity walked back to Dani as she watched the ambulance drive away. "How is he?"

"Okay enough to order me around. How's Cindi?"

"She's out cold. Looks like she was drugged. I called for a second ambulance." Verity paused. "She's lucky. If you and Powers had arrived a few minutes later, she would have been Michael's third victim."

Dani called dispatch and arranged for the crime scene team to convene at Cindi's house. She also directed that patrol deputies take shifts guarding Cindi at the hospital. Then, she called Connie and told her what had happened.

The second ambulance arrived. Dani followed the paramedics inside the back door of the house. Cindi was lying on the garage floor, in front of the laundry room door. The paramedics checked Cindi's vitals, loaded her onto the gurney, and took her out the front door to the ambulance.

Paget, Tipton, Martell, and Ryder came into the house carrying their crime scene gear. Dani had them start processing for evidence in the kitchen and laundry room. She went outside and met up with Nash and Mercer. Dani showed them where Michael had gone into the woods. "Look for blood. Powers shot him in the shoulder."

An hour later, Connie called Dani on her cell. She walked outside and answered the phone. Connie said, "The bullet went clean through. It missed all of Cliff's vital organs. But it cracked one of his ribs. The doctor said he can probably go home the day after tomorrow."

"I should be there with him."

"Don't bother. They gave him somethin' for the pain, and he's sound asleep. I've never heard such snorin'."

"Thanks for letting me know."

Nash emerged from the woods and motioned Dani over. He said, "We found blood."

Dani retrieved her crime scene kit from the SUV and followed Nash. She looked down at the drops of red and said, "I'll process this. You guys keep searching."

"Roger that."

Dani took the blood she collected inside the house to the evidence technician. Ryder said, "I'll send this to the state crime lab first thing. Hopefully, that psycho's in the DNA database."

Dani nodded. "Thanks. How's it going in here?"

"Slowly. The crime lab will have to eliminate Cindi's fingerprints from all the ones we're processing. And, there's no telling how many people have been in her house or who they are. I'll go see Cindi and get a list of names. Follow up by getting a set of their prints."

"That would really help. We have so much to do, it's hard to keep up with all of it." Dani paused. "If you guys are okay here, I'd like to go to the hospital and check on Cindi and Cliff."

Ryder said, "Go. We've got this."

Dani loaded her things into the SUV and drove to the Kalispell Regional Medical Center. There were no available spaces in the lots surrounding the hospital, so Dani parked at the yellow curb in front of the main entrance. Dani held out her badge to the older woman at the information desk and asked which rooms Powers and Cindi were in.

When Dani walked into Powers' room, a nurse was taking his blood pressure, even though he was asleep. Dani said, "He's my partner."

The nurse smiled at Dani. "We're taking good care of him. The doctor said he's going to be fine."

Dani continued to watch Powers as she said, "Thanks." The nurse left, and Dani moved next to the bed. She stood there, looking down at him.

Connie came into the room carrying a cup of coffee. "I called his sisters. They're on the way."

Dani nodded. "I'm going to see if Cindi's awake."

"I'll stay here until Powers' sisters arrive."

Dani didn't have to search for Cindi's room. Looking down the corridor, she could see a uniformed officer sitting next to the door. She recognized Deputy Willie Baines as she got closer. "Hey, Willie."

Banes stood. "How's Powers?"

201

"According to the doctor, he'll be out of here in a couple of days," Dani said. "They gave him something, and he's asleep right now. How's Cindi doing?"

"Doc said she's fine. She's awake. I imagine you want to talk with her." Banes knocked lightly on the door, then opened it and stood aside for Dani to enter.

Dani introduced herself to the beautiful young woman lying in the hospital bed. Dani saw that Cindi had a small bruise on her left cheek. Other than that, she seemed physically unharmed.

Cindi said, "One of the nurses told me that you and your partner saved me. Thank you. I'm sorry your partner was hurt."

"No thanks necessary. We were just doing our jobs. And, he's going to be fine." Dani took a notepad and pen out of her handbag. "Do you feel up to telling me what happened this morning?"

When Cindi nodded, Dani pulled the guest chair next to the bed and sat down.

Cindy said, "I got ready for work, as usual. When I opened the door into the garage, he was standing to the side of it. Up against the wall. He pointed a gun at my head and told me to be quiet. I was so startled that I jumped away from him. I turned around and, stupidly, started slapping at him. He backhanded me." Cindi touched her cheek. "I fell down, and he jumped on top of me.

Then, he stuck me in the neck with something. That's the last thing I remember until I woke up here."

"Did you see his face?"

Cindi shook her head. "No. He had on a black ski mask. But I saw his eyes. They were dark brown."

"What was he wearing?"

"Blue jeans and a blue sweatshirt. And, he had on brown leather gloves."

"Do you live with anyone?" Dani asked. "We need to eliminate their fingerprints."

"No. I live alone. I'm not even dating anyone."

"Okay. One of our officers will come by later to get a list of people that have been in your house." Dani took a business card out of her handbag and handed it to Cindi. "If you think of anything else, give me a call."

"I will," Cindy said. "And, thanks again for saving my life."

Dani smiled and left the hospital room. Baines was still on guard duty. She thanked him and walked back to Powers' room. From the doorway, Dani saw that Powers' sisters were there, so she didn't go inside. Dani went back to the nurse's station and asked to see Cindi's doctor.

The tag on her scrubs identified the nurse as Rita. "He's gone home for the day. Is there something I can help you with?"

"The sheriff's department will need a copy of Cindi Bowers' blood tests. We need to know what she was drugged with."

Rita said, "We already got those back." She took a folder out of the metal file rack that was sitting on the countertop and said, "Hang on a minute." Rita took the folder to the copy machine, opened it to the correct page, and made a copy. Handing the paper to Dani, Rita said, "It was ketamine."

"Thanks." Dani slipped the copy of the blood tests into her handbag. Before she got back into the SUV, Dani called Paget. "I'm leaving the hospital now. I'll be back at Cindi's in twenty minutes or so."

"We already finished there. We're on our way back to the Center."

"In that case, I'll head back to the office." Dani arrived as Paget and Ryder were walking out the front door. She thanked them for their help and went to her office. The area was completely empty. Dani sat at her desk and straightened the items on top of it. She looked at the photographs of Josie, Terra, and Cindi, wondering who would be next. Dani decided to go home and spend some time with Bo. She took her keys out of her handbag and walked down to the lobby. Tate was standing at the building's front entrance.

Dani asked, "What are you doing here? Were you waiting for me?"

Tate said, "Yes. I thought maybe I could take you out to dinner." He shrugged. "I know you haven't been eating."

"That's very nice of you to offer." Dani shook her head. "But I just want to go home."

"I understand."

Dani continued outside. Since the parking lot was almost empty, she could see that there wasn't anyone lurking around. She checked inside the Jeep before unlocking the door and getting inside. As Dani drove home, she constantly looked in the rear view mirror to assure herself that nobody was following her.

When Dani pulled up to her house, she miscalculated the timing of the garage door opening. She had to wait a few seconds before driving in. Dani berated herself. It had been years since she'd blown her entrance into the garage by that much time. As always, she waited for the garage door to completely close before unlocking the Jeep.

Once inside the house, Dani followed her compulsive checking of the locks on all the doors and windows. Satisfied, she opened a bottle of Chardonnay and filled a wine glass. Dani turned on the vinyl record player, started a jazz album, and sat on the couch sipping wine. Bo licked Dani's empty hand. Eyes closed, Dani listened to the smooth notes of the saxophone and stroked Bo's soft ears. She tried in vain not to think of Powers lying on the ground, bleeding.

Suddenly, Bo growled loudly. He ran to the front door and began barking. Dani quickly set the wine glass on the coffee table and drew her Glock. She saw Tate Howland cross in front of the picture window. When the doorbell rang, Bo's barking became frantic. Dani quieted Bo and told him he was a good boy. She holstered her gun, disarmed the alarm, unlocked the door, and opened it.

Tate smiled and held both arms out in front of him, a white bag in each hand. "Chinese." He walked into the house, set the bags on the island, and began removing white cartons.

Dani locked the door and armed the security system. She went into the kitchen and got out two sets of cutlery, plates, and napkins. Dani reached across the island and set them next to the take-out boxes.

When Dani's cell phone rang, she looked at the caller identification and saw that it was Kevin Mercer. Dani swiped the answer icon and listened. Then she said, "Everything's fine.

Thanks for checking." Dani ended the call and told Tate, "That was your tail."

Tate paused for a second, then said, "After today, I'm glad to know that someone's watching you."

Dani walked into the kitchen and threw her arms around Tate's neck. Her tears wet the front of his shirt. Tate held Dani until she stopped crying. She dried her face on a paper towel and took a wine glass out of the cabinet. Dani filled it with Chardonnay and handed it to Tate. She retrieved her glass from the living room, refilled it, and gulped a large mouthful.

Dani rubbed her hand over the wet spot on Tate's shirt. "Sorry about that."

"Don't be sorry." He placed his hand on Dani's to still it. "But, I can't think straight with you rubbing my chest." Dani jerked her hand back and blushed. Tate smiled mischievously and pulled her into an embrace. He sweetly kissed Dani before saying, "Let's eat before it gets cold."

Dani shoveled half of each container onto her plate. "I just realized that I haven't eaten all day."

"Glad I could help."

"You did. And, not just with the food." Dani sipped wine. "I guess I was more affected by Powers getting shot than I knew.

I'd been holding all my feelings inside. Until you showed up, that is."

CHAPTER 9

Dani and Tate had talked until almost midnight. He'd told her about his marriage. She'd related more about how her stepfather had treated her.

It wasn't until Dani was almost at the Center the next morning that she realized Michael hadn't called the night before. As soon as she entered her office, Dani asked Verity, "Do you think he's seriously injured?"

"I can't think of any other reason why he wouldn't call you."

Dani said, "I hope he dies from the wound."

"I prefer that he lives."

"Why? Because you'll get a promotion when he's arrested?" Dani realized that Richards and Webb were watching her. She looked at them and shrugged. "Well, it's true, isn't it?"

Verity said, "Perhaps. But, it's also true that if we don't catch him, I'll get all of the blame."

Dani found it hard to muster even a little sympathy for Verity. She took a deep breath to calm herself. "So, what's our next move?"

Verity said, "Even though it's mandatory that doctors report gunshot wounds, we should still check emergency rooms and clinics in the area. In case they haven't gotten around to reporting it."

Dani said, "I'll visit them in person. Better chance of getting an honest answer if they have to look into a face. I'll start at the Kalispell hospital."

Tipton said, "Hey, give him my best."

"Mine too," Martell said. "Tell him we'd come visit, but we're too busy talking to Aunt Alice, who thinks her nephew Tommy in Austin is the bible killer."

Dani drove her Jeep to the hospital and parked in the visitor's area. She decided to visit Cindi first, but the duty nurse said that Cindi had already checked out. So, Dani went to see Powers, who she found sitting up in bed, eating breakfast.

"Hey, Cliff. How are you feeling today?"

"Ready to get the hell out of here and eat something that doesn't taste like cardboard." Powers pushed the food away.

Dani took the tray and set it on the side table. "Has the doctor been here today to see you?"

Powers shook his head. "He said I can go home tomorrow."

"That's great."

"How's Cindi?"

"She was released this morning. I'll go to her house later and check on her."

"What's going on with the case?"

"You must have got Michael pretty good. We found blood drops in the woods, and he didn't call me last night."

"I'm glad to hear it. I know his calls have been hell for you."

Dani shrugged. "I'll live. Hopefully, we'll catch him soon, and it'll be over."

Powers coughed. He winced, putting a hand on his side. "Amen to that."

"I better get going. I'm on my way to the local hospitals and clinics to check if a man came in with a gunshot wound. I'll come by early tomorrow and drive you home."

"Thanks. I'd appreciate that."

Before Dani left the hospital, she checked at admittance for any patients with gunshot wounds. They had no record of any, so she made her way to the four urgent care centers in Kalispell. None of them had treated a gunshot wound either. Dani drove the seventeen miles to North Valley Hospital in Whitefish. With no luck there, she checked at the urgent care. When Dani struck out at it, she considered driving the fifty-one miles to Eureka. But she figured that if Michael had been able to make it that far, he would have driven the additional thirteen miles into British Columbia. Just to be sure, she called the medical clinic in Eureka. They had no record of a gunshot wound. Dani knew another possibility was that Michael had found a doctor who does work off the record.

As Dani was driving back to Kalispell, her cell phone rang. She pulled off the highway onto the shoulder and answered. "Detective McKenna."

"Dani, this is Alyce. I went to your office, but Verity told me you were in the field."

"What's up?"

"Thought you'd want to know that the lab results on Terra's car found an unidentified hair. Male. Short. Dark brown."

"Terra's fiancé was blonde, so it can't be his. If it is Michael's, it'll be one more nail in his coffin."

"Lab's still running the DNA on the blood you processed at Cindi's. As soon as they finish, we'll know if the hair is a match or not."

"Thanks for calling, Alyce."

"No problem."

Dani disconnected, pulled onto the highway and drove the remainder of the way back to Kalispell. Before returning to the Justice Center, she went to Cindi's house. The patrol deputy on guard duty nodded at Dani as she pulled onto the driveway. Cindi opened the front door before Dani rang the bell.

"Detective, hi. How can I help you?"

"I just stopped by to check on you and see how you're doing. I went to the hospital earlier, but you'd already left."

"Please, come in." Cindi closed and locked the door after Dani entered.

Dani sat in the living room chair that Cindi indicated. "How are you doing?"

"Honestly, I'm scared and nervous. I don't feel safe here anymore. I'm having a security system installed. They'll be here this afternoon. When I explained what had happened, they squeezed me into their schedule."

"That's good. I hope it helps you feel better."

Cindi chewed on one of her fingernails.

Dani said, "How you're feeling is perfectly normal in this situation, but I highly recommend that you see someone. It'll help."

Cindi nodded. "I hadn't thought of that."

"If you don't know someone, I can give you the name of a great doctor."

Cindi said, "I'd appreciate that. Hang on and I'll get a piece of paper and pen."

Dani wrote Doctor Ellison's information down and handed it to Cindi. "You have my card. You can also call me anytime." Dani rose to leave.

"Thanks. I appreciate that," Cindi said as she walked Dani to the front door.

Dani could hear the deadbolt slide into place as she moved down the sidewalk to her Jeep. On the way to the office, Dani drove through the drive-in window at Starbucks and got herself a venti mocha latte.

As she walked into the Center, Dani saw Tate standing in the lobby, speaking with a man. Dani could feel her face flush when Tate's eyes met hers. She tried to cover her embarrassment by sipping coffee. The man was so busy talking that he didn't even notice when Tate's focus shifted. Tate gave Dani a small smile, then turned back to the man.

In the detectives' office, Dani gave everyone an update on Powers' condition and her visits to the hospitals and clinics.

Agents Richards and Webb had finished reviewing all the CCTV footage. They'd seen several trucks that were the right make and model. But none of them had been driven by a man matching the sketch of Michael.

Martell said, "We've received four tips on Michael from non-crazies that need to be followed up on. But Tipton and I are stuck here. The calls are still coming in." As if to punctuate the point, Martell's phone rang. He rolled his eyes and answered.

Verity said, "Richards and Webb. You take those potential leads and check them out.

"Roger that," Richards said. The two agents retrieved the information from Tipton after he disconnected the call he'd been on.

Connie came into the office with Terra's autopsy report. "The lab made it their number one priority."

Verity held out his hand. "I'll take it." He silently read the report for a few minutes. Verity said, "Ms. Tucker had ketamine in her system." He flipped pages and silently read. "The lab found the same fibers that were on Mrs. Aiken's body." Verity paused, then said, "The fibers could be from something Michael's transporting the women in or from an article of clothing that he's wearing."

Martell ended the phone call he's been on and said, "I have one more potential tip."

Dani stood and said, "I'll take it." As had become her habit, Dani checked inside her Jeep before getting in. She drove to the address on Washington Street and spoke to the older man that had called in the tip. He had the ruddy complexion and bulbous nose of a man who liked his alcoholic beverages. As they spoke, Dani could smell alcohol on the man's breath. It quickly became evident that this was a waste of time. Dani felt sorry for the man. People like him sometimes called in because they were lonely and wanted company. She thanked the man for speaking with her. As Dani was walking back to the Jeep, her cell rang. It was dispatch. "McKenna."

Wallis Boone said, "Patrol called. Cindi Bowers is missing."

Dani sprinted to her Jeep as she asked, "What do you mean she's missing?" Dani started the vehicle and backed out of the driveway, tires squealing.

"You should get over to Cindi's house and talk to Ed Abrams. He was on duty."

"I'm on my way. Does Verity know?"

"Yeah. We've been directed to call him first. So, I did."

"Thanks, Wallis." As Dani drove she checked intersections before she blew through them, not stopping at any red lights or stop signs. She arrived at Cindi's house less than five minutes after the call from dispatch. Verity hadn't arrived yet.

Ed Abrams walked over and met Dani as she was getting out of the Jeep.

Dani asked, "What happened?"

Abrams pointed to the van parked in the driveway. "A guy driving that Kalispell Alarm van came to install Cindi's security system. He had overalls on with their logo, and Cindi said she was expecting him." Abrams kept talking as he and Dani walked inside the house. "About fifteen minutes after the guy got here, I decided to check on his progress, and Cindi was gone. He would've had to take her out the back door."

Dani said, "He must not have been injured as badly as we thought. Probably had his truck parked in the alley."

Abrams rubbed his double chin. "Crap. I can't believe this happened on my watch. I should've stayed inside. But Cindi told me everything was fine and that I would only be in the way if I stayed inside."

"Call it in. Get everyone available to start searching. Have patrol stop and search every white Ford F-150 they see." Dani walked through the house. Nothing seemed amiss or out of place. She went out the back door to the back gate. She looked both directions down the alleyway but didn't see anyone. Dani went back inside. "I'm going to drive around and start looking for Cindi. Stay here and wait for Verity."

Dani drove to the alleyway and followed it to the next intersection. She went down every street, getting further and further away from Cindi's house. After thirty minutes, Dani saw a patrol unit slowly approaching in the oncoming lane. She recognized Todd Nash in the drivers' seat. He gave her a small salute as they passed. It was getting dark by the time Dani gave up searching the area. She decided to look for Michael on the peninsula across the lake from her house. Dani drove the loop of Island Drive. She followed every private road until it ended. Then, she got out of the Jeep and walked around. At five of the houses, the occupants came out and confronted her. Dani showed them her badge and told them to go back inside while she searched. She didn't find any sign of the truck or Michael.

As Dani drove the short distance home, she thought about Cindi. The overwhelming sense of failure Dani felt took her breath away. The first thing Dani did when she got inside the house was to fill a wine glass with Chardonnay. She was sitting on the couch, drinking wine and thinking about the unpredictability of the future, when Bo started barking.

When the doorbell rang, Dani drew her Glock and moved to the front door. She looked out the peephole and saw Tate standing there. A smile crept across her face. Dani quieted Bo. She disarmed the security system, unlocked the door, and opened it.

"Burgers and fries," Tate said, holding up a large bag. He reached his other arm around Dani's waist and pulled her close. Dani turned her face up towards Tate's and kissed him. "Mmmm," he said, "I could get used to that greeting."

Dani holstered her gun, locked the door, and armed the alarm. She took the bag from Tate. Dani reached inside and removed one of the burgers. She stuffed a wad of fries into her mouth, closed her eyes, and moaned. "So good."

Tate laughed. He set the bag on the countertop and took out his burger. "You didn't eat all day again, did you?"

Dani took a bite of the double meat and cheeseburger and shook her head. As she chewed, she went into the kitchen and poured Tate a glass of wine. She retrieved hers from the coffee table. The two sat at the island. Dani took an enormous bite of burger. It was almost too big for her to chew. Tate reached over and wiped a dab of mayo off of the corner of Dani's mouth with his thumb. She chuckled, almost choking. When they had finished eating, the two took the wine to the living room and sat on the couch.

Tate said, "I heard about Cindi. I'm sorry."

"I feel sick about it. I let her down."

"You're not responsible for what happened. You can't be everywhere and do everything. You're only one person."

Dani was quiet for a full minute. "When my dad shot himself, I felt responsible for that too. I thought that if I'd been nicer to him or if I hadn't misbehaved, he wouldn't have killed himself."

Tate put his arm around Dani's shoulders and kissed her forehead. "Did your mom know you felt that way?"

"No. I didn't tell anyone. I didn't even tell the psychiatrist that I saw for ten years after I came to live with my Grandma."

"Thank you for trusting me enough to tell me."

Dani turned toward Tate and kissed him. They explored each other's mouths until both of them were breathing faster. Dani unbuttoned Tate's shirt and splayed both hands out on his chest. Tate leaned back onto the couch, pulling Dani on top of him. She could feel that Tate was as excited as she was. Dani trailed her tongue down the side of Tate's neck, causing him to moan. He flipped over, placing one knee between Dani's legs. Then Tate kissed her as he unbuttoned her shirt. Dani's mind was blissfully blank until Tate put his hand between her legs. She pushed against him. "Stop. Stop."

Tate sat up. "I'm sorry. I got carried away."

Dani buttoned her shirt. "No. I'm the one who should apologize."

Tate tilted Dani's head up with his finger. "Hey. I can wait as long as you need." He picked up Dani's glass of wine and handed it to her. He took a drink of his wine and smoothed his hair.

Dani said, "There's something I need to tell you."

Tate looked into Dani's eyes. "Okay."

Dani looked away and took a drink of wine. "I've only been with one man. And, that was a long time ago."

"I hope you know by now that I like you a lot. I'm not in a hurry." Tate stood up and took Dani's hand. "Come on. Walk me to the door." Tate gently kissed Dani good night.

Dani was checking the locks when her phone rang. She looked at the screen. Michael was back.

"Did you think I would let you take one of my chosen women away from me?"

Dani could hear Cindi moaning in the background. She disconnected the call. Michael immediately called back, but Dani didn't answer. She pressed the power button and turned the phone off.

CHAPTER 10

Dani went straight to the hospital early the next morning to take Powers home. While they were waiting for the paperwork, she briefed him on Cindi.

Powers said, "I can't believe Michael had the balls to take her with a uniformed officer right there."

"Ed feels bad. But it could have happened to any of us."

A nurse came in with the paperwork for Powers. She gave Powers the antibiotic and pain medication he would need to take at home. Then, the nurse had him get into a wheelchair so she could take him to the main doors. Dani went ahead of them and brought her Jeep around to the front. She opened the passenger door and waited for Powers to gingerly climb in. Dani helped him with his seat belt, closed the door, and went around to the drivers' side. She drove slowly, trying to avoid jostling Powers.

Powers kept his hand on his side where the bullet had entered. "How's Verity?"

"A pain in the ass. He keeps insisting that I know something about Michael."

"Wish I could be there to keep him off your back." Powers grimaced when the Jeep's tire hit a small pothole.

Dani glanced sideways at him. "Don't get any ideas about coming back until you're completely healed up. There are three FBI agents, three sheriff's detectives, and all our patrol deputies on this. There's nothing you can do."

"Gee. Thanks. I feel so needed."

Dani chuckled. "Sorry. I didn't mean it like that."

"Do me a favor and call me regularly. Let me know what's happening."

"Glad to." Dani parked in the 'no parking zone' in front of Powers' apartment building. She set her sheriff's department' placard on the dash.

Powers got out of the Jeep before Dani could get around to the other side. "I got it," he said. They moved slowly down the sidewalk. Powers bent forward a little at the waist. By the time they got to the door of his apartment, there was a sheen of perspiration on his forehead. Dani helped Powers get settled on the couch with the television remote. "I'm good here. Get going. You need to help find Cindi."

Dani drove to the Center, locked her Jeep, and went inside. Verity and a uniformed state police officer were standing in the foyer. Several other people were milling around in small groups, whispering. Dani stopped and looked at Verity, confusion clear on her face.

Verity nodded toward Dani and approached her with the officer. Verity said, "Detective Danielle McKenna, you're under arrest for obstruction of justice during a federal investigation."

Dani glared at Verity. "Are you crazy? What are you doing?"

The state police officer held out his hand. "You'll need to surrender your firearm and your badge."

Dani pulled the chain of her badge holder over her head and handed it to police officer. She removed her Glock from the holster and held it out to him, handle first."

The murmuring in the room intensified as the state police officer handcuffed Dani's hands behind her back. People on the second-floor started coming downstairs to see what was happening. Tate was in the midst of them.

When Tate saw Dani being Mirandized by Verity, he pushed his way through the crowd and rushed forward. He grabbed Verity by the arm. "What do you think you're doing?"

Verity pulled his arm away and said, "This matter does not concern you, Deputy Attorney Howland."

Dani shook her head at Tate to wave him off. He stood still and watched helplessly as Dani was taken down the corridor to the adult detention facility.

Dani was processed into the jail by a female detention officer with a curvy figure. When the officer saw Dani's name, she asked, "Are you Cliff Powers' partner?"

Dani nodded. "Do you know Cliff?"

The woman smiled. "A little."

Because Dani was an officer of the law, she was put in solitary. The inside of her cell smelled of an antiseptic cleaning product. Rage and adrenaline filled her, making her jittery. Dani paced back and forth in her cell for what seemed like forever, but was actually only an hour.

A male detention officer came to Dani's cell, handcuffed her, and escorted her to an interrogation room. He directed Dani to sit on a metal chair at the table in the room. Then, he connected Dani's cuffs to a steel ring on the table. The officer stood against the wall by the door, not making eye contact. Five minutes later, Verity came in and sat across the table from Dani. He excused the detention officer. Dani tried to keep her face void of all emotion.

Verity laid a folder on the table, opened it, and slid a photograph toward Dani. He said, "I told you that I'd find what you've been lying about. You kept vital information from the FBI, resulting in the hindrance of an investigation." He tapped the photograph. "That's a picture of you when you were seventeen. After you escaped from your kidnapper... from Michael."

Dani didn't look at the photograph. She continued to stare at Verity without speaking.

"Only your name wasn't Danielle McKenna then. It was Justine Maxwell. Your birth father's last name was Maxwell. McKenna was your mother's maiden name."

Someone knocked on the door of the interrogation room. Verity's eyes showed anger at being interrupted. He practically stomped to the door, throwing it open.

Tate stood in the doorway. "I'm Detective McKenna's attorney. There will be no further meetings with her unless I'm present." Tate tried to enter the room, but Verity blocked him.

"You're a county attorney. You can't represent her."

"Not anymore. I quit. And, I registered as her attorney. Let me repeat. There are to be no meetings with my client unless I'm present. Now, if you'll excuse us, I'd like to speak with Detective McKenna alone."

Verity went back to the table. He angrily picked up the photograph, shoved it inside the folder, and turned to leave. As Verity was walking out, he intentionally bumped Tate with his shoulder.

Tate told the officer standing outside that the handcuffs weren't necessary. The guard removed the cuffs and took them with him when he left. Dani rubbed her wrists. Tate closed the door behind him.

Dani stood. "What did you do? You can't quit. Not because of me."

Tate reached Dani in two long strides. He wrapped his arms around her.

Dani pushed away from him. "You can't quit your job!"

Tate took Dani's hands in his. "I care more about you than I do any job. End of discussion."

"No, it's not. What were you thinking?"

"I'm going to start my own practice. You're my first client. Now, sit down and let's discuss the charges."

Tate sat on the chair that Verity had vacated. Dani slid back onto her chair. She could feel the cold metal through the orange scrubs that she was wearing.

Tate set the briefcase he'd brought with him on the table and opened it. "Verity has charged you with obstructing the investigation by means of deception, thereby preventing the FBI from apprehending the perp." Tate looked at Dani. "Attorney-client privilege. Anything you tell me is confidential."

Dani looked down at the table. She picked at the peeling top coating. "I don't know who Michael is. But there's something I should have told you. I tried to the last time you were at my house. But, I chickened out. I was afraid that you wouldn't want me after you heard what had happened."

"I'd kiss you right now to show you that nothing could keep me from wanting you. But I can't be involved with my clients. So, that kiss will have to wait until you're cleared of the charges."

Dani took a deep breath and blurted out the details of waking up in the cinderblock room and being hit by her kidnapper. Dani rubbed her temple. "That's how I got this scar." She told Tate about having sex with her kidnapper every day for the two weeks that she was held a prisoner. Dani kept her eyes on the tabletop as she said, "He didn't rape me. I acquiesced."

"Of course you did. You did what you had to in order to survive."

Dani looked up at Tate, amazed that his reaction wasn't one of revulsion.

Through clenched teeth, Tate said, "I'd like to kill that bastard."

"Too late. I already did. There was a towel rack bolted to the wall in the room where I was kept. Little by little, I was able to unscrew the bolts. I had to be careful and hide my hands because my fingernails tore and bled."

"After sex, he always stayed in the room awhile, lying on the blanket on the floor. The day I escaped, I put my clothes back on and went to the toilet. I couldn't believe it when I realized that he'd fallen asleep. I guess he'd gotten complacent, thinking I was docile and submissive. I knew I might never get another chance like that."

"I quietly pulled the loose bolts out of the wall. The towel rack was one of those cheap metal kinds. I tiptoed back to where he was lying and hit him on the head with it. The towel rack just bent in half. He got to his hands and knees and I shoved one of the bolts into the back of his neck. He always wore this scarecrow hood, so I couldn't see where the bolt went in. But he pulled it right back out. While he was screaming and rubbing at his neck, I jammed the other bolt into his thigh. That one went in deep, and he couldn't get it out. He'd thrashed around so much that the eye holes in the hood were out of place and he couldn't see. I grabbed the keys out of his pants pocket and ran for the door. After I got out of the room, I locked him inside of it."

Tate placed his hand on top of Dani's. "That was incredibly brave of you."

"The cinderblock room had been built inside of an old wooden barn. I ran out the door of the barn and kept blindly running. I didn't have any shoes on. Trees and bushes tore at my face and clothes, but I didn't stop. I had no idea what direction I was going. The only thing I could think about was getting as far away as possible. In hindsight, that was stupid because I had the keys. He couldn't get out."

"At some point, I stopped running and started walking. I walked all through the night. I only remember that it was cold. Sometime the next day I came to a gravel road and started walking down it. A while later an old man driving a beat up truck drove by. When he stopped and got out, I thought he was there to take me back to the room. I started screaming. He got back in his truck, turned around, and drove off. Half an hour or so later an old woman drove up in the same truck. She wrapped a blanket around my shoulders and got me into the vehicle. The only thing I remember about her was that she had dark liver spots on her hands. I watched her hands as she drove me to the hospital in Missoula. She told the police that I'd said that's where I lived."

"Come to find out, my parents hadn't even reported my kidnapping. My stepfather said he thought it would be bad for business." Dani's eyes filled with tears. "And, my dear mother went along with him."

The look on Tate's face turned angry. "What was wrong with those people?"

"Of course, a police report was filed when I got to the hospital, and it all came out. But my stepfather's rich and powerful, so no charges were filed against him or my mother."

Tate shook his head in dismay. "I'm so sorry, Dani."

"I was in the hospital for two days. I arranged for my grandmother to pick me up when I was discharged. I've never seen or spoken to my parents since. I legally changed my name from Justine Maxwell to Danielle McKenna."

Tate asked, "What about your sheriff's department application?"

"I didn't lie. On the application, I disclosed that I had used the name Justine Maxwell in the past. It wasn't flagged as an issue."

Tate nodded. "Good. The sheriff went along with Verity's nonsense. We don't want to give him any justification for firing you."

"I never saw the kidnapper's face. I don't know who he was. But, I know that he's dead. I had the key to the door. He couldn't have gotten out of that room. So, he couldn't be Michael. I didn't tell Verity about the kidnapping because it's not relevant to the case." Dani paused. "You and my psychiatrist are the only two people who know what happened. But now everyone will know."

"Not if I can help it. I'm going to issue a motion to dismiss on the grounds of failure to state a claim. If that doesn't work, I'll have a motion to suppress ready to hand to the judge."

Dani reached across the table and took Tate's hand in hers. "Thank you."

He squeezed her hand. "I'll be back as soon as I can." Tate stood up and opened the door, telling the guard that they were finished.

Dani was handcuffed and led back to her small cell. The anger that she'd felt earlier was gone. In its place, fear and panic were starting to set in. Dani knew she couldn't let those feelings take hold. She started jogging in place. When Dani was winded, she got down on the concrete floor and began doing push-ups. When Dani's arms started shaking, she began jogging in place again. The adrenaline started to have the desired effect of overshadowing Dani's anxiety. She kept exercising until the female detention officer that had checked her in came back.

The officer said, "There's someone here to see you."

"I'm not supposed to talk to anyone without my attorney present."

The woman smiled. "You're going to want to see this person. Sorry about the cuffs, but I'll be dismissed if I don't use them." The officer took Dani back to the same interrogation room where she'd seen Verity and Tate. The woman removed the cuffs and opened the door. "I can only give you fifteen minutes."

Dani's forehead was creased in confusion as she walked into the room. Then she saw Powers sitting at the table. He grunted in pain as he pushed himself out of the chair.

"What are you doing here?" Dani said, "You should be at home."

Powers put one arm around Dani and quickly hugged her. "With my partner in jail? To hell with that."

Dani chuckled. "At least sit down, you big dope." She shook her head. "You and Tate are quite a pair." Dani explained about Tate resigning.

"Way to step up and be a man."

Dani rolled her eyes. "I don't need rescuing." She sat on the opposite chair.

234

"Yeah, yeah. We know." He paused. "I got a look at the charges. What does Verity have?"

Dani went through the story about her kidnapping and name change again. After, she said, "I should have told you about my past a long time ago. I'm sorry."

"No worries. I can understand why you didn't. No more secrets going forward, though. Okay? Partners don't keep secrets."

Dani nodded. "No more secrets."

The female officer knocked on the door and opened it. "Sorry, Cliff. You need to go before someone sees you."

Powers said, "Thanks for doing this, Lucy. I owe you one."

Lucy smiled. "And I know how you can pay me back. I'll show you when I come by tonight."

As Lucy was putting the cuffs back on, Dani turned and raised her eyebrows at Cliff. He smiled mischievously and shrugged. Lucy led Dani back to her cell. Dani said, "Can I ask how long you and Cliff have been seeing each other?"

Lucy said, "A little over a month. Sorry, but I asked him not to tell anyone yet."

Dani smiled. "I understand."

Dani alternated between pacing and exercising in the cell for another six hours. A lunch tray with a plastic spoon was brought to her, but the thought of eating turned Dani's stomach. True to his word, Tate got the charges against Dani quickly dismissed. As she was walking down the corridor from the jail to her office at five thirty that evening, Dani tried to talk herself out of going ballistic on Verity. She didn't want to waste any more time. Dani wanted to concentrate on finding Cindi and stopping Michael.

When Dani walked into the room, Verity stood and said, "Detective McKenna, I have been directed to apologize to you for having your arrested."

Dani looked at Verity and waited.

After a few seconds, Verity stuck his chin out and said, "I apologize."

"Thank you. I appreciate the apology." Dani looked around the office and saw that the other four men were all staring at her. She couldn't imagine what Verity had told them. Dani looked each person in the eye and squared her shoulders. "I have something I want to say. When I was seventeen, I was kidnapped. The man that took me wore a hood, so I never saw his face. After two weeks, I escaped. I locked the kidnapper inside the cinderblock room where he'd been keeping me. The police never found the place where I was held. The man that kidnapped me couldn't have gotten out of that room because I had the key. So,

236

he couldn't be Michael. What happened to me is not connected to this case. And, it was private, which is why I didn't disclose it."

Martell said, "You don't have to explain anything to me. I never doubted you." He looked Verity squarely in the eyes.

Tipton said, "Same here."

Dani nodded at them. She took a deep breath, then asked, "Where are we on finding Cindi?"

Martell said, "This afternoon we ruled out the last two tips. And, the phones have stopped ringing."

Dani said, "Last night I searched the entire peninsula across from my house. There was no sign of Michael or his truck." She turned toward Verity. "Is patrol still staking out River Road?"

Verity nodded. "They have been. But tonight I've assigned Agents Richards and Webb to take over. Detectives Tipton and Martell will patrol Island Drive tonight. You are not to go anywhere near either area. You are to go home and wait for Michael to call. Under no circumstances will you terminate the conversation before he has."

Dani shook her head at Verity in exasperation. She turned and walked back out of the office. Before she left the parking lot, she called Tate. He was at home. "Will you please come over tonight?"

He teased. "I thought you'd never ask. I'll pick up dinner and be there shortly."

On the way home, Dani stopped at a liquor store and bought two cold bottles of her favorite Chardonnay. When she got home, she opened one and poured two glasses. Tate arrived shortly after. Dani opened the front door and kissed him. She pulled him inside and started to unbutton his pants. Tate captured her hands and drew them up to his mouth. He kissed each one.

Dani frowned. "What's wrong?"

"I don't want you to do this because you feel that you owe me. When we make love, I want it to be because we care about each other. If we had sex now, both of us would probably feel bad about it after. So, let's wait. Alright?"

Dani thought about what Tate had said, then nodded her head. "Okay."

Tate kissed Dani on the forehead. "I got tapas. Lots of different kinds." He picked the bag up from where he'd dropped it on the floor.

As they ate, Tate relayed what he'd said to the judge about Dani's charges being frivolous. "Judge Bartel was going to call Les Michaels and let him know that one of his agents needed to be reined in. I don't think Verity's career is going to be the same after that call."

Dani told Tate about Verity's apology. Then she said, "I'm glad that my past is out in the open. This case is stressful enough without trying to hide it." Dani smiled. "Enough about me. Tell me what your plans are for your business."

Tate talked excitedly about opening a private practice. "I've always wanted to do more pro bono work. Now I'll be able to. And, I can pick my own clients."

The two finished eating and moved to the couch. They sipped wine and discussed where Tate should look to rent office space, and about hiring an assistant.

Dani didn't realize it was so late until Michael called. Tate held her hand as she put the phone on speaker.

"It was very rude of you to hang up on me last night."

"I didn't like listening to Cindi suffer."

There was silence for a second. "I can understand that. It was insensitive of me to call from inside that place. From now on, I'll call when I'm outside."

Dani perched on the edge of the couch. Maybe she could get Michael to reveal something about where he was keeping Cindi. Dani asked, "Do you have to go outside? Couldn't you go into another room?"

"There's only one room."

"You know, there are a lot of bears in the woods around Kalispell. It might be dangerous to go outside at night."

"I'll be careful. Thank you for being concerned about me. I love you, Dani. I'll talk to you again soon." Michael disconnected.

Tate looked at Dani and said, "Until I heard that, I didn't realize how hard this case must be on you."

"It's definitely brought up things I'd rather not think about," Dani said. "But I actually feel better than I have in quite a while. Telling you, and having you react the way you did, helped me shed some of the guilt I've been hauling around all these years."

Tate leaned in and sweetly kissed Dani. She savored the feel of his lips on hers. Bo interrupted the moment by licking the side of their faces. Tate laughed. "I think he's jealous. He's never had to share you before. Or, he could be telling me that it's time to go home." Dani walked Tate to the door. They kissed good-night.

Now that Dani was alone, she couldn't keep from thinking about Cindi. Visions of Cindi being tortured ran through her mind. She paced from one end of the house to the other four times. As Dani started the fifth round, she stopped and said, "Come on Bo, let's go for a ride."

Dani didn't know exactly where she was going, but she couldn't sit at home and do nothing. Michael had said that he was keeping Cindi in a one-room structure in a wooded area. The Flathead and Kaniksu National Forests made up the vast extent of the woods around Kalispell. But it was unlikely that Michael had a building on forest land. Lone Pine State Park bordered the city on the west, and there were several properties on the outskirts of the park. So, she decided to start there.

When Dani got to Foys Lake Road, she rolled the windows down. Bo stuck his head out and sniffed the air. Dani reached over and rubbed his neck. "When this case is over, we'll do this more often, buddy." Bo wagged his nub of a tail and licked Dani's hand.

Dani drove slowly, listening for anything unusual. She turned down every side road and looked for single room structures that were secluded. When Dani encountered one, flashlight in hand, she would look inside. If the door was locked, Dani would walk around the building until she found a window or even a crack to look through. Dani drove and searched until four thirty in the morning, ending near the airport. There was no sign of Michael, his truck, or Cindi. Dani knew it had been a long shot, but she had to try something. She couldn't just sit at home and do nothing while Cindi suffered.

CHAPTER 11

Dani set her alarm for six and flopped on top of her bed fully clothed. When the alarm started to beep, she felt like she'd only been asleep for a minute or two. Dani took her clothes off and stood under the pulsing spray of the shower for a few blissful minutes.

When Dani went into her walk-in closet to get dressed, she found that all her work clothes were dirty. Dani turned the laundry basket upside down and dumped the contents onto the tile floor. She picked up a shirt and sniffed it. She did the same with a pair of khaki cargo pants. Dani decided they weren't too bad. She took them to the laundry room, threw them into the dryer with a dryer sheet, and set it for a five minute touch-up. Dani tapped her foot as she waited. After a long two minutes, she removed the clothes. Dani took the slightly freshened pieces back to the bedroom and dressed. She gave Bo a hug and drove to the Center, stopping for coffee at her usual place.

As Dani walked down the hallway, she felt a little twinge of sadness that Tate was no longer upstairs. The feeling seemed odd to Dani, as she'd avoided him for so long. Dani sat at her desk and looked at wooded areas near Kalispell on google maps.

Tipton walked in. "Hey, Dani."

Dani looked up at him. "How did it go last night?"

Tipton shook his head. "No sign of Michael."

Dani told him what Michael had disclosed about his location, and where she'd searched.

Verity came into the office. He must have overheard because he said, "I told you to stay home last night."

"No, you didn't. You told me not to go near Island Drive and River Road. I wasn't near either of them. And, I waited until after Michael had called."

Martell and the two FBI agents showed up in a group. The three tried to ignore the tension in the room. Dani repeated the details about the phone call and her idea to search single room dwellings in wooded areas.

Addressing Verity, Webb said, "It's not a horrible idea, boss. We're out of other options. We can't search title records because we don't know Michael's real name. Same with DMV records for his truck. We could each take a potential area around Kalispell."

Verity said, "It would be a crapshoot. As you go further and further out of Kalispell, the potential wooded area gets larger and larger." Verity motioned with his hand. "All the way up to Eureka, over to Libby, down to Missoula. On and on."

Martel said, "I'm sure the sheriff would approve some available patrol units to join in. We could break up the area into small sections. Each person could take one section."

Tipton said, "There are five of us. If we get the eight patrol deputies that are on the crime scene team, that makes thirteen. We could knock it off pretty quickly."

Webb said, "You could be here, boss, coordinating the searches. When someone finishes an area, you could move them to a different one."

Richards said, "It's better than doing nothing, boss."

Verity looked around at the people in the room. After a couple of seconds, he said, "Alright. We can give it a try. I'll speak with Corporal Tirrell about the patrol deputies. One of you get the maps we need."

Within forty-five minutes the search party was assembled in the detectives' office. They gathered around a large map that Martell had bought at the Visitor Center. Verity assigned different sections to each person. After, he said, "I'll call the city police and other sheriff's departments to let them know that you might be in their jurisdictional area. This is an FBI led team, so that shouldn't be a problem."

Dani was assigned the area from West Glacier south to Nyack. Dani searched every one-room structure that was surrounded by

244

woods. It was slow and tedious going, but she was glad to be busy. At one o'clock Dani stopped at a little diner and bought a large coffee to go. She added plenty of sugar and cream for whatever energy they might provide. Then, Dani remembered that she hadn't eaten breakfast or lunch again today. Thinking of Tate, she added a ham and Swiss cheese sandwich to her order. Dani ate the sandwich in the SUV.

Alyce Ryder phoned as Dani was backing up in the parking lot of the diner. "Hi, Alyce."

"I wanted to give you a heads up that the DNA from the blood and hair didn't match. So, no help there."

"That's alright. We have enough on Michael without the hair. The blood alone will be enough."

"One other thing. I eliminated the fingerprints of the people that Cindi remembered having been in her house. I also eliminated them from the new batch of prints that we took after she was kidnapped the second time. I ran the unidentified prints thru the database, but there weren't any hits. If Michael left any prints, they're not in the system."

"Thanks, Alyce. I really appreciate all your help. You're the best." Dani placed her phone back in the holder attached to her belt. She adjusted her Glock to accommodate the seat belt better and drove back to where she'd last searched.

By three thirty, some team members were starting to call in on their radios. They had finished searching their areas and were looking for a new assignment.

Dani was in the SUV finishing her cold coffee when Kevin Mercer came on the radio. Mercer was breathy as he said, "I think I found something."

Dani tossed the cup on the passenger seat and picked up her radio. She clicked the talk button as she started the vehicle. "Where are you?"

"I'm north of Pinnacle. Back in the woods by the Flathead River. There's no road to this place. I almost missed it."

Dani said, "Text us the coordinates."

"This is Verity. Do not approach. I'm on my way. Wait until I arrive to approach."

Dani hit the lights and siren and sped the eighteen miles down Highway 2. When she turned off onto a dirt road leading to the coordinates, she shut them off. The road was muddy from the rain earlier that afternoon. Dani could see the tire tracks that Mercer's vehicle had made. The SUV fishtailed, warning her to slow down. When the road ended, Dani saw that Mercer was waiting for her.

Mercer rushed forward as Dani approached. As soon as she stopped the SUV, Mercer opened the driver's side door. He pointed toward the river. "I couldn't see inside, but I could hear a woman moaning."

Dani drew her gun, took the safety off, put her hand over the slide, and chambered the first round.

Mercer said, "Are we waiting like Verity said?"

"No way."

Mercer drew his gun and chambered a round. "Glad to hear it."

Dani keyed her radio to transmit. "Verity. I'm here with Mercer. He heard a woman in distress. We're going in."

"Absolutely not! You are to wait for me!"

"If it is Cindi, she could be dead by the time you get here. We can't wait." Dani turned her radio off and tossed it in the open door of the SUV. She told Mercer, "Turn your radio off, so it doesn't give us away." Dani could hear Verity screaming her name before Mercer turned the button on his radio.

"The cabin's about two hundred yards down this path." Mercer went to his vehicle and withdrew a black steel battering ram. "In case the door's locked."

247

"Lead the way." Dani followed Mercer down a narrow path. Both of them turned sideways in an attempt to avoid snapping the branches of the encroaching brush. Ten feet out from the cabin, Mercer stopped and crouched down. Dani knelt down beside him. She listened, frowning when she didn't hear anything. Dani whispered, "Is there a back door?"

Mercer shook his head. "No windows either."

Dani asked, "You ready?"

Mercer nodded. He holstered his gun and gripped the battering ram by the handles. Dani went ahead of him, Glock held ready to fire. At the door, Dani nodded. Mercer stepped up to it and heaved the heavy metal ram. The splintering door frame sounded like an explosion. The door swung into the room, banging against the wall.

Dani rushed inside, gun held before her. The metallic smell of blood assaulted Dani's nostrils before her mind could comprehend what she was seeing.

Cindi was lying on a stainless steel autopsy table that was covered in her blood. A large metal bucket sat under the table's drainage hole. A steel cart with two deep shelves sat next to the table. It held a bone saw, a hooked hammer, a chisel, kitchen scissors, and several scalpels.

Standing over Cindi, holding a long serrated knife was Michael. He spun around when the door flew open.

Dani took a firing stance. "Drop the knife!"

Michael was wearing a butcher's apron, covered in rust-brown blood. He smiled and set the knife on the cart next to Cindi. "Justine, it's so nice to see you again."

Dani saw Mercer glance her way before he rushed forward. Mercer barked, "On the ground, asshole!" Michael did as he was ordered. Mercer used double cable ties to quickly restrain Michael's hands behind his back.

Dani went to Cindi and checked her pulse. "She's still alive." Dani called for an ambulance on her radio.

Cindi's breasts had been completely removed and were sitting on the cart. She had five long lacerations on her abdomen and genital area.

Dani said, "Get that piece of shit out of here. And, bring back your trauma kit."

Mercer nodded. He pulled Michael up off the floor and led him by one arm out the door.

As Michael crossed the threshold. he said, "I'll see you soon, Justine."

Mercer's elbow connected with Michael's nose. "Oops. Slipped."

Michael licked the blood from above his mouth and smiled. "Mmmm."

Dani took her shirt off and carefully covered Cindi with it. The light blue cotton instantly started to wick the blood, streaking it red. Dani took Cindi's hand and leaned closer to her ear. "Hang on Cindi. Hang on."

Mercer returned. Dani took the trauma kit from him and set it on the table next to Cindi. Dani held out her hand to Mercer. "Give me your shirt."

Mercer didn't even bother with the buttons. He grabbed both sides of the collar, pulling hard. The buttons made a tinkling noise as they hit the concrete floor. Mercer shrugged out of his shirt and handed it to Dani.

Dani said, "I'll stay here with Cindi. Wait at the end of the road and lead the medics to the cabin."

"Roger that." Mercer turned and left again.

Dani removed a pair of latex gloves from a pocket on her cargo pants and pulled them on. She opened the trauma kit and removed every butterfly bandage that she could find. Dani took her shirt off of Cindi, opened one bandage after the other, and did her best to close the slashes on Cindi's torso. Then, she opened the packages of gauze and used them to cover the worst of the wounds. She draped both shirts over Cindi's torso. Dani picked Cindi's hand back up and squeezed it. "You're going to be okay. You hear me. You're going to be okay."

Verity, Richards, and Webb arrived a few minutes before the ambulance. When the three walked inside, Webb was the only one that said anything. He uttered two words. "Dear Lord." Verity called dispatch and requested the crime scene team be sent to process the cabin.

Mercer led the emergency medical team to Cindi, where they immediately checked her vitals and began intravenous fluids. Dani let go of Cindi's hand when the medics moved her onto their portable stretcher.

Dani told the others that she was going to follow the ambulance, and asked Mercer if he would book Michael.

"It would be my pleasure."

Verity said, "I'll ride with Deputy Mercer. I want to question Michael after he's booked. Webb and Richards, you oversee the collection of evidence."

Dani, Mercer, and Verity trailed behind the medics through the brush to the ambulance. As Dani passed Mercer's patrol car, Michael puckered his lips and made kissing motions toward her.

Mercer walked up to the window and slapped it with his open palm. Michael leaned his head back and laughed.

Dani ignored Michael and continued walking to her SUV. She turned on her lights and followed the ambulance as it sped to the hospital in Kalispell. Dani parked in front of the main doors and ran around to the emergency entrance. The head nurse asked her to take a seat in the waiting room until the attending physician could speak with her. As Dani walked down the corridor, she called Powers. When he answered, she said, "We got Michael. And, Cindi's alive."

Powers whistled, forcing Dani to hold the phone an arm's length away from her ear. Powers said, "Tell me. Don't leave anything out."

Dani relayed the day's events, trying to remember as much detail as she could. Occasionally, Powers would interrupt to ask a question. When Dani finished, she asked, "How are you feeling?"

"Right now I feel great."

"I'll call you when I hear how Cindi's doing." Dani paced in the hallway outside of the waiting room. When she finally saw the doctor coming, she hurried toward him.

The doctor stepped to one side of the hall to allow others to pass by. He asked, "Are you the person that treated her wounds?"

Dani nodded.

"You saved her life. If she'd had any more blood loss, she wouldn't have made it."

"How is she?"

"None of the wounds were deep enough to cause damage to her internal organs. The danger now is infection, but we've got her on a heavy dose of antibiotics. Barring any complications, she should make a full recovery." The doctor paused, shaking his head. "I've never seen anything like that before. I guess you have in your line of work."

"Unfortunately, I've seen other cases of rape. But not the mutilation."

The doctor shook his head. "There's no sign that Cindi was raped."

Dani drew in a deep breath and let it out. "That's great news."

"We'll keep Cindi sedated for the rest of the day and night. You can see her tomorrow."

"Thanks for letting me know how she's doing." As Dani walked to the SUV, she called Powers back and gave him the update on Cindi's prognosis.

Dani drove back to the Justice Center, wondering how Cindi would cope psychologically. Dani knew from experience that it took a long time to heal mentally when your world was no longer a safe place to live. Each person handled trauma differently. Some suffered from severe anxiety, others felt guilt, shame, and self-blame. Some exhibited anger, irritability, and mood swings. Dani had felt all of those and more. Her way of coping was to withdraw. And, to become a detective who could help other victims. Dani smiled and said out loud, "Today was a good day."

When Dani arrived at the Center, she headed straight for her office. Connie saw her coming down the hallway. She came out from behind her desk and shuffled over to Dani. Connie said, "I'm so proud of you."

Dani nodded. "Thanks. But it was a team effort."

Connie patted Dani on her arm and glanced at Corporal Tirrell's office door. "For the record, I didn't agree with how the sheriff handled your arrest. He should've stood up for you."

Dani shook her head. "None of that matters now. We saved Cindi, and we got the bad guy. That's all that matters."

Connie gave Dani a quick hug and went back to her desk.

When Dani walked in the door of her office, she saw that the search team members were all there. Todd Nash noticed Dani first. He stood up and started clapping loudly. The rest of the team followed. Dylan Doherty produced an ear ringing whistle. Dani smiled and held up both hands to stop the noise. When it had subsided, Dani said, "Kevin's the one who found Cindi. He deserves the credit, not me."

The team members turned toward Mercer and started clapping. When the applause died down again, Mercer said, "Thanks, Dani. But the search was your idea. I just executed it." Everyone shouted agreement.

Dani held up her hands again. "I talked to Cindi's doctor a few minutes ago, and she's going to recover." The team members cheered. Dani said, "Knowing Cindi, she'd like to meet you, Kevin. She can have visitors tomorrow."

Mercer nodded. "I'll go see her."

People slowly trickled out of the office. Some were headed home, others to resume their regular duties. They all patted Dani and Mercer on the back and mumbled words of praise as they left.

Nash was the last to go. He shook Dani's hand and said, "You're an amazing detective."

Dani blushed, then smiled. "Thanks for saying that." She stood in the doorway, looking at the pictures of Josie, Terra, and Cindi for a few seconds. Dani slowly walked back down the hallway and to her Jeep. This time she didn't check inside before getting in. Before Dani left the parking lot, she called Tate. "I feel like celebrating. Want to come over later?"

"Of course. What are we celebrating?"

"I'll tell you all about it when you get there."

"Okay. What kind of food do you want me to pick up?"

"Surprise me."

"Is there any kind of food that you hate?"

"Liver. I hate liver." Dani involuntarily shivered. "Yuck."

Tate laughed. "No liver. Got it. See you soon."

~~~

As soon as Dani got home, she took a shower. She felt like she needed to wash away the lingering filth of Michael. Dani shampooed her hair, lathering it twice. She put on sweatpants and a sweatshirt. Dani was still drying her hair when Tate arrived. Bo's barking alerted her. She rushed into the living room, disarmed the security system, and unlocked the front door. Dani flung it open and happily announced, "We got Michael!"

Tate put his arms around Dani, picked her up, and twirled her around. She laughed. When Tate set Dani back down, she quickly kissed him and said, "This calls for a toast!" Tate put the grocery bag he was carrying on the counter. Dani closed the front door after him and went into the kitchen. She poured two glasses of wine and handed one to Tate. Holding her glass up, Dani said, "Here's to no more late night phone calls. To no more Bible quoting notes. And, most importantly, to no more victims."

Tate said, "Here, here." The two clinked glasses and sipped wine. Tate set his drink down and rubbed his hands together. "I got two ribeye steaks." He pointed at the chairs at the breakfast bar. "Sit and tell me all about it while I cook."

Dani hopped onto one of the bar stools and told him about the day. Tate smiled and nodded as he listened. He rubbed the meat with spices, then chopped vegetables for a salad. When Dani finished talking, Tate asked, "How do you like your steak cooked?"

"Medium rare, please."

"Me, too." Tate leaned across the bar and kissed Dani's cheek. "Where do you keep your bowls?" Dani pointed. Tate filled a bowl with salad and took it to the dining room table. In a smaller bowl, he whipped olive oil, lemon juice, and spices into a frothy dressing.

Dani set the table, then put one of her favorite classical jazz vinyl records on the player. When the timer for the steaks went off, Tate forked them onto a large platter, which he then set next to the salad. He said, "Let's eat."

Dani unconsciously hummed along with the swing and blue notes as she came back to the kitchen. She added some wine to both glasses and took them to the table.

Tate held up his wine glass. "My turn to toast." Dani smiled and picked up her glass. Tate said, "To an intelligent and tenacious detective, a tough person, and a gorgeous woman. To you."

Dani felt her face flush as she said, "Thank you." Dani made yummy noises as she chewed the first bite of meat. "Tell me about your office hunt. Did you find anything acceptable?"

"I decided on a small house that's two blocks from the Justice Center and court. It has an entry that's large enough for a secretary and a waiting area. It has two office spaces. I'll use one as a conference room. It also has a small kitchenette and bathroom. Rent's affordable and there's an option to buy, if I decide I want to do that later." Tate shrugged. "It's well maintained and it looks nice inside and out."

"That's wonderful. I'm so glad for you." Dani leaned toward Tate and kissed him. "Sit. I'm doing dishes tonight." Dani cleared the table, loaded the dishwasher, and scrubbed the grill." She could feel Tate watching her the entire time. When she turned from the sink and saw the smoldering in his eyes, Dani slowly walked to him. Never taking her eyes from his, Dani straddled Tate's legs and sat on his lap. She placed both arms around his neck and brought her lips to his. Tate's lips parted. Dani explored his mouth with her tongue. Tate put his hands on her bottom and drew her hips forward. Dani closed her eyes and leaned her head back as Tate trailed his tongue down her neck. She reached down to the hem of her sweatshirt and pulled it over her head. She let it drop to the floor. Dani pulled Tate's shirttails out of his pants, then unbuttoned it. Dani could feel Tate turn hard under her. She pushed the shirt over Tate's shoulders and ran her hands down his chest to his belt buckle. She unfastened the belt and the top button of his pants.

Tate moved his hands to the back of Dani's knees and stood up, carrying her. Dani told Bo to stay. She ran her tongue along the side of Tate's neck as he moved into the bedroom. Gently, he laid Dani down on the bed. Tate pulled Dani's sweatpants over her hips and down her legs. He unzipped his pants and took them off. The two eagerly explored each other's body with their hands and mouths. Dani was panting as Tate removed her underwear, then his own. Dani closed the distance between their bodies and breathlessly whispered, "I want you." Tate tasted every inch of Dani. When he finally entered her, Dani raised her hips to meet him. Tate moaned. They made love quickly and passionately.

After, Tate held Dani in his arms. She looked at him and, with a mischievous grin, asked, "Are you tired?"

"No."

Dani climbed on top of him. "Good."

CHAPTER 12

Dani opened her eyes the next morning and smiled, remembering the night before. She sighed contentedly, turned her head, and looked at Tate. He was lying on his side, still asleep. Dani tried to sneak out of bed without waking him, but as she sat up, Tate held her wrist and said, "Come back. I want to snuggle with you." Dani wriggled toward Tate. He put his hand on her backside and pulled her close. Dani chuckled and said, "Snuggle, huh?" Tate smiled. "It's not my fault that you're so damn sexy." They made love again, then took a shower together taking turns lathering each other with soap.

Dani was drying Tate's back with a large fluffy bath towel when her cell phone rang. She handed the towel to Tate, grabbed another off the rack, and wrapped it around herself. Dani looked at the caller identification. "It's Verity." She swiped the answer icon. "McKenna."

"Michael says he won't talk to anyone but you."

Dani sighed. "I'll be there as soon as I can." She ended the call and told Tate about Michael. "Now, Verity needs me."

"He's a jerk. There's no doubt about that." Tate paused. "I don't like the idea of you having to be around that sick SOB again."

"Neither do I, but I don't have a choice. We still don't have any idea of Michael's real identity." Dani paused. "I'd also like to know why he chose me."

Tate nodded. "I understand. I still hate thinking of you being anywhere near him."

The two dressed and left the house through the garage. After Tate had driven away, Dani sat in her Jeep thinking about how she might get Michael to tell her what they needed to know. She stopped for coffee on the way, arriving at the Center at eight-twenty.

Verity, Richards, and Webb were in the detectives' office. Verity was pacing back and forth. As Dani entered the room, he said, "Let's go."

Dani said, "Good morning to you too." She shoved her handbag in the bottom drawer of her desk and followed Verity down the corridor to the jail. Neither said anything to the other. Verity had arranged for Michael to be waiting in an interrogation room. Dani stood and looked in the one-way mirror at Michael. He was cuffed to the table, staring at the mirror.

Dani walked to the interrogation room's door, took a deep breath, and turned the knob. She nodded at the guard standing inside. "You can leave us." Dani sat across the table from Michael.

He watched as the guard closed the door behind himself. Then, Michael turned his head and smiled at Dani. "Justine. I can't tell you how wonderful it is to see you again."

"My name's not Justine."

Michael leaned forward in his chair. "I know that you changed your name. But, you'll always be Justine to me."

"Justine doesn't exist anymore. I'm Dani. Justine was weak. I'm not." Michael continued to smile at Dani. She said, "You wanted to talk to me. So, what did you want to say?"

"Do you want to know what my name is, Justine?"

Dani pushed her chair away from the table and stood up. She calmly walked toward the door.

Michael frowned and asked, "Where are you going?"

Dani turned back to him. "Do you want to talk to me or not? If not, I have better things to do than sit here while you play games."

"Sit down... Please."

Dani sat back on the metal chair, but she didn't pull it up to the table. She folded her hands in her lap and looked into the dark holes that were Michael's eyes.

"You know. I was amazed that you found me. I can't figure out how you did it."

"I'll tell you how, if you tell me your real name."

Michael smiled. "I like that idea. We'll trade. One question and answer. You go first."

Dani figured she didn't have anything to lose. "The last time you called me, you said that you were in a one-room house in the woods."

"Very smart."

Dani said, "Now it's your turn. What's your real name?"

"You don't remember me, do you?"

Dani crossed her arms over her chest. "You haven't answered my question."

Michael leaned forward in his chair again. "My name's Michael." He laughed. "Isn't that perfect?"

Dani narrowed her eyes. "Your whole name."

"Michael Gersch."

Outside, Verity called Webb on his cell phone and gave him the name. "Find out everything you can about this guy and bring it to me. ASAP."

Michael said, "Now it's your turn. Do you remember me?"

Dani shook her head. "No. Where would I know you from?"

"We went to high school together." Michael leaned back in his chair. "I'm not surprised that you don't remember me. I adored you, but you didn't know that I existed."

Dani asked, "How would I have known that you adored me?"

Michael frowned. "I said hi to you every time I saw you."

Dani's brow furrowed. "Did I ignore you?"

"You would say hi. But you never smiled or stopped to talk to me."

"Is that why you killed Josie and Terra and almost killed Cindy? Because you were angry at me?"

"They were beautiful, like you. And, conceited. And, rich. Just like you."

Without another word, Dani stood up, walked to the door, opened it, and walked out.

Michael said, "Where are you going? Justine! Come back here. Don't leave, Justine!"

Verity met Dani in the hallway. She didn't speak to him. Dani rushed back to her office, took her handbag out of the desk, and left the building. She drove her Jeep straight to Powers apartment. When Dani knocked on the door, Lucy answered.

Lucy said, "Hi. Come in. Cliff's in the living room." Dani trailed behind Lucy to the small space. Powers pushed himself out of the lounge chair he'd been sitting in. "Hey. What's up?"

Lucy went to him, kissed his cheek, and said, "Call me later." She smiled at Dani before leaving the apartment.

Powers looked at Dani. "You want some coffee?"

Dani shook her head. She sat on the edge of the couch. "I'm the reason those women were kidnapped and tortured."

Powers lowered himself back down into the brown leather chair. "How do you figure that?"

Dani told Powers about her meeting with Michael.

"So what? Every high school boy had a crush on a girl that didn't feel the same way about him. And, they don't go around ten years later, killing women that look like their crush. The guy's a psycho."

"This is all so messed up. I don't know what to think or how to feel."

"Maybe you should take a few days off. Go see someone. I mean, hell, after what you went through as a teenager and now this. Any sane person would be feeling out of sorts."

Dani thought about the idea of not being in the office for a couple of days. It sounded blissful. "I'm going to do just that." Dani smiled. "So... tell me about Lucy."

"I will, if you'll tell me about Howland."

"Deal."

Powers and Dani talked for another half hour. Dani drove back to the office and spent the rest of the day doing paperwork. She typed up her interview with Michael, and updated the Murder Book. She also put together the information that the county attorney's office would need to file charges against Michael. When Dani had finished, she gave the forms to Connie for formal submission upstairs. Then, she went back to her computer and logged herself as off duty for Saturday and Sunday.

Dani drove to the hospital to visit Cindi. When she got to Cindi's room, Dani saw that a nurse was inside. Dani stood in the hall until the nurse had finished. Cindi was hooked up to a fluid and antibiotics drip. An older man and woman sat in visitor's chairs next to the bed.

267

Dani knocked lightly on the wood door. "Do you feel up to a visitor?"

Cindi smiled. "I'm so glad you're here. Please come in." The man and woman stood up as Dani entered the room. "Mom. Dad. This is Detective Dani McKenna. She's the one that saved my life. Dani, this is my mom and dad, Frank and Silvia Bowers."

Dani shook hands with both of them. "Nice to meet you."

Silvia Bowers said, "We cannot thank you enough for saving our daughter's life."

Frank Bowers' head bobbed up and down in agreement.

Dani said, "Actually, I didn't find Cindi. That was one of our patrol deputies."

Cindi smiled and said, "We met Kevin this morning. He came by to see how I'm doing. He's so sweet."

Frank Bowers said, "Officer Mercer told us that you came up with the idea for the search. The doctor also told us that you kept Cindi alive by tending to her wounds."

Dani blushed and changed the subject. "How are you feeling?"

"I'm incredibly grateful to be alive." Cindi shrugged. "Boobs can be replaced. A good plastic surgeon can erase the scars from the cuts. But, I can't be brought back to life. And, I want to do a lot more during that life. I want to fall in love, get married, and have kids. Sit on the porch in a rocking chair and watch my grandkids play. I'll be able to do all that, thanks to you."

Dani said, "And the rest of the team."

Cindi held out her hand. Dani crossed the room and took it. Tears welled in Cindi's eyes. "I could hear you talking to me, and I could feel you holding my hand. It kept me there."

A tear rolled down Dani's right cheek. "You're an amazing woman." She let go of Cindi's hands and brushed the tears away. "I should go. Let you rest. Keep in touch."

Dani said goodbye to Cindi and her parents. Dani could hear them talking and laughing as she walked down the corridor. Dani felt a pang of sadness that she didn't have that kind of parent-child bond. She started the Jeep, then called Doctor Ellison and made an appointment for the next day. Before she put the vehicle in drive, she called Tate and told him that she'd taken the weekend off.

"Neither one of us have to work," Tate said. "We could spend the weekend together... if you'd like to, that is."

"I'd like that. I'm cooking dinner tonight. Come over about six."

"You cook?"

"Don't sound so scared."

"What I meant was... You cook!!"

"Right. Nice try, Howland. But you can't extract your foot from that."

Tate laughed. "I'll bring wine."

"Bring your stuff so you can stay over."

"Roger. Bring PJs."

Dani mischievously said, "I'm certain you won't need those. See you later tonight." She smiled all the way to the store. As Dani was entering the supermarket, she realized that it had been a month since she'd last bought groceries. She stocked up on all the essentials – toilet paper, Chardonnay, and coffee. Dani purchased the ingredients for lasagna, fresh vegetables for a salad, and a loaf of crusty Italian bread. She also bought an assortment of olives, marinated artichoke hearts, and cheeses for an antipasto plate. Dani's stomach grumbled and her mouth watered in Pavlovian response.

The first thing Dani did when she got home was to turn on the oven and start the water heating for the lasagna noodles. She put her hair up in a low, messy bun and took a quick shower. Then, she changed into jeans and an aqua colored zip-up cardigan. Dani tied her grandmothers' old red gingham apron around her waist and started cooking.

Bo watched every move Dani made, drool eventually escaping from the corner of his mouth. Dani looked at him and said, "What? I know I haven't cooked anything in a long time. But, you don't need to give me away with that look."

When Tate arrived, the lasagna had twenty minutes more to bake, and the garlic bread was ready to pop under the broiler. Dani unlocked the front door and opened it. Tate walked inside, backpack in one hand and bottle of wine in the other. "Mmmm, what smells so good?"

"My grandmother's lasagna. She was a great cook." Dani shrugged. "I'm a half-decent recipe follower. Hope you weren't looking for a girlfriend that would find the way to your heart by cooking."

Tate stopped mid-stride to the kitchen. Dani almost bumped into his back. He turned and looked at her.

Dani frowned. "What? What's wrong?"

Tate smiled widely, teeth and dimples showing. "You just called yourself my girlfriend. Well, sort of. But, I'll take it."

Dani thought about what she'd said and blushed.

Tate set the bottle of wine on the countertop and the backpack on the floor where he stood. He put his arms around Dani's waist. "Besides, you've already found your way into my heart." Tate drew Dani into a long kiss.

Breathless, Dani broke away. "Will you open the wine while I finish the salad?" She tossed the vegetables into a large bowl and set it in the refrigerator. Dani picked up the antipasto plate and two small appetizer dishes. "Let's have this on the porch."

Tate poured two glasses of wine and followed Dani outside. They put everything on the round bistro table and sat in the cushioned chairs. Dani took a cracker off the plate and piled three different kinds of cheese onto it. As she was chewing, Tate leaned over and brushed a crumb off of the side of her cheek. Dani smiled at him.

The sky above was clear, twinkling with a million stars. Moonlight reflected off the smooth surface of the lake. Dani thought the distant mountain slopes looked like the craggy planes of a face. She sighed. "I've missed being able to come out here... to just sit and enjoy the peace." Dani closed her eyes and listened to the night sounds of crickets chirping and frogs croaking.

"It's beautiful here," Tate said. "I can see why you like it so much." He paused. "I realize that I don't know what kinds of things you like to do."

Dani leaned back in the chair. "Hmmm. Let me think. I like reading and watching movies. I have eclectic tastes with both. I like fantasy, sci-fi, action, and crime mysteries mostly. Definitely not horror. I get enough of that at work." Dani picked up a black olive and popped it into her mouth. "What about you?"

"I like all kinds of outdoor activities. Hiking, canoeing, waterskiing, sailing... Do you like any of those?"

Dani was glad that Tate couldn't see her face because she was embarrassed. She drank wine and ate an artichoke heart, stalling. Finally, she said, "I might as well admit it. I've never done any of those things."

Tate's brow furrowed. "Why not?"

"My dad was always working when I was young. My stepfather's idea of roughing it was to go to a five-star hotel for the weekend and get massages, facials, and manicures."

Tate took Dani's hand and held it. "Maybe we could do some of those things together."

Dani smiled at him. "That would be nice." She ate more crackers and cheese. "Tell me about your family."

"My parents have been married for thirty-five years." Tate chuckled. "My mom says she got pregnant with me on their wedding night. I have one younger sister, Evelyn. She's a third grade school teacher in Billings. That's where I was born. My parents still live in the same house that they bought when they were first married. They're great. Still madly in love."

"What do they think of your career change?"

"They're supportive. Of pretty much everything I do."

Dani looked into her glass. "Did you tell them why you quit?"

"Yes. They're proud of me. And, happy that I've met someone I care about. It's been a long time."

Dani looked at the lake and sipped wine. "I had that kind of support from my grandmother. But, she's gone." Dani stood up. "No more sad talk. Let's eat before I consume this entire plate of cheese."

They ate at a leisurely pace in the dining room, talking about Tate's new practice. When they finished, they cleared the table and curled up together on the couch.

Suddenly, Tate said, "I forgot to tell you. I found a paralegal!"

"You did? Wow! That was fast."

"Her name's Serena Garber. I lucked out. My cousin Quinn is a friend of hers. The firm she worked for dissolved. She'd been unemployed for two weeks and was thrilled to get my offer. I can't pay her as much as she was making. But, she likes the idea of working for a single attorney and running the office. So, she accepted."

"That's wonderful. When does she start?"

"First thing Monday morning."

Dani chuckled. "Sounds like you need to get busy setting up your office. Unless you want her to sit on a folding chair at a folding table, that is."

"I was hoping you'd come shopping with me tomorrow. I don't know a damn thing about decorating."

"I have an appointment at nine in the morning, but after that, I'm all yours."

Tate rubbed his hands together. "Great. It'll be fun to do it together." He stood, took Dani's hands, and pulled her up. With a playful grin, Tate said, "I know something else we can do together that's fun."

Dani laughed and let herself be led to the bedroom.

~~~

The next morning Dani made coffee while Tate showered. When he'd finished, she took his place.

They sat outside and drank coffee. Bo sniffed the entire porch in case anything had ventured onto it during the night.

Dani said, "That appointment I have this morning is with my long-time psychiatrist."

Tate looked at her with concern. "Are you alright?"

"Actually, I'm better than I've been since the kidnapping. But, I have a lot of baggage that I need to keep working on."

Tate leaned across the side table between their chairs and kissed Dani on the forehead. "You're an amazing woman."

Dani blinked several times. "I just told you that I have issues and you call me amazing." She shook her head. "Most guys would be running for the hills right now."

"You're not alone. We all have issues. That's part of being human. I'm not worried about it." Tate took Dani's hand in his. "And, I'm not going to run away."

They finished their coffee. Dani went to her appointment, and Tate went home to work on a business plan for his practice. They arranged to meet at a local bakery at ten-fifteen.

Dani was almost eager to see Doctor Ellison. Dani felt that she'd made more progress in the last week than she had in the ten years prior.

As they talked, Doctor Ellison agreed. "I'm very proud of you. You're an amazing woman."

Dani grinned. "That's what Tate said a few minutes ago."

"Smart man."

When Dani's hour was up, she agreed to start coming regularly again. Outside, Dani took a deep breath of the crisp air. She felt relieved that she didn't need to check the inside of the vehicle or worry about notes being on its windshield.

Dani found herself smiling as she drove to the bakery. She hadn't felt happy for a long time. Dani ordered a huge cinnamon roll covered in gooey icing and coffee. Tate got a poppy seed scone and coffee. They took Dani's SUV shopping because it had more room than Tate's Subaru. Even though Dani was driving, she finished eating first. She licked her fingers and washed the sticky sweetness down with coffee. "I'm stuffed."

"Good. It could be a long day of shopping."

Before they'd left the house, Dani and Tate had looked on-line at the furniture stores in town. There were only two that had everything Tate needed to set up his practice. They stopped first at the most promising one and went inside. The salesman almost started salivating when he heard that Tate was ready to buy so much furniture.

The website for the store indicated that delivery would be scheduled a week after the furniture was purchased. Tate looked the salesman in the eye and said, "If I buy everything here, I need it delivered today. If you can't arrange that I'll go elsewhere."

"Let me go check with my boss real quick. I'm sure it can be arranged." When the man returned, Dani thought he looked like he might skip across the floor. "Yes, sir. We can do that. No problem."

Dani and Tate decided that contemporary was the best style choice, as it was more sophisticated than the others. They agreed on a rich dark finish accented with satin nickel hardware. With that decision made, they picked all the pieces in the same brand and style. They chose two desks, each with six drawers for storage. They decided on eight large bookcases, eight tall filing cabinets, and two black wingback office chairs. They bought a long oval table and eight chairs for the conference room. Then they went to the living room area. There they chose a black leather sofa and two matching chairs, all with slim arms, a tightly padded back, and tapered legs. They quickly picked out a coffee table and two end tables in the same contemporary style and color as the rest. Several lamps with cream shades completed the purchasing spree. Tate paid with a credit card and arranged to have everything delivered at two that afternoon.

As they exited the store, Dani said, "That was easy. Now to the office supply store."

As Dani drove them to the closest store, Tate found a website that had a list of office supplies needed to start a business. When they went inside, Tate pulled up the list on his phone. They got two carts at the entrance and started at the top of the list. In the end, shopping for office supplies took longer than buying the furniture had, and they needed a third cart to hold it all.

They got to Tate's office ten minutes before the furniture was due to arrive. He said, "Come on. I'll give you a quick tour." Tate opened the front door and led Dani by the hand through the empty rooms, showing her which one was going to be his office and which would be the conference room.

Dani smiled. "I like it. It's not so big that it's impersonal and it's not crowded either."

Tate looked out the front window and rubbed his hands together. Excitedly, he said, "The furniture's here."

Dani helped Tate check each piece for any damage as it was brought inside. Tate directed the delivery men where to place the furniture. After the men left, Dani and Tate walked through each room, tweaking the placement of a few pieces. Then, they started unloading all the office supplies from the back of Dani's Jeep. They carried the items into the correct rooms. But they didn't unbox any of it because it was six-fifteen and they were both hungry.

Tate said, "Let's go out to dinner."

Dani sighed. "That sounds good. Let me wash up real quick." She went into the small bathroom and washed her hands and face with cold water. When Dani came back out, she said, "We need to go to a grocery store tomorrow." She motioned toward the bathroom with her chin. "No toilet paper or towels to dry your hands on." Dani shook her still wet hands, then wiped them down the side of her pants.

Tate draped his arm over Dani's shoulder. They walked to the front door, then out to the Jeep. Dani started the vehicle, then asked, "Where do you want to eat at?"

"I was thinking of Bert's Burgers."

"That sounds great."

They drove the short distance downtown and couldn't believe their luck at finding two empty stools at the counter. Bert's was nothing more than a small grill inside an old-time pharmacy. Most people took their food to-go because there were only nine stools at the counter.

Dani and Tate ordered double meat double cheeseburgers with fries and root beer. They watched Bert do his magic, listening to the sizzle and pop of the meat on the grill. The fries were made from fresh skin-on potatoes. Dani wondered how Bert knew just when to remove them from the hot oil so that they were perfectly crisp on the outside. The burgers and fries were served on large plates. Dani and Tate concentrated on eating, neither talking. When they were nearly finished, Tate said, "I'm glad you're not one of those women that eats nothing but salad."

Dani chuckled. "Me, too."

Tate pushed his empty plate away. "You know. This is the first time that we've been out together in public."

Dani was well aware of that fact. "I know." She shrugged. "I don't like people knowing about my personal life. Full disclosure, though. I told Cliff about us."

Tate smiled. "I'm glad. I'd hate to run into him and have to pretend that nothing was going on between us."

"I'm trying to be more open with him. I haven't been in the past, and I feel bad about it. As he keeps reminding me, he is my partner."

~~~

On the way to Dani's house she dropped Tate at his car. When the two arrived, they took Bo for a walk along the lakefront. Tate

281

motioned toward Bo. "I think I'm making progress with him. He didn't threaten to eat me when we got back tonight."

Dani smiled. "He's a great watchdog. I couldn't sleep after my Grandmother died. I was afraid of being alone in the house. That's why I got him. I've always felt safe with him around."

"His bark alone would scare most people."

"That's exactly what I intended."

When Bo ran out of energy, Dani and Tate went back to the house and curled up on the couch with a glass of wine. Dani started yawning, so they went to bed early. However, neither went to sleep until an hour later.

The next morning they were both still full, so they skipped breakfast. Dani made coffee, which they took in insulated mugs to the grocery store. Along with bathroom products, they bought a coffee maker, cups, coffee, cream, and sugar. Tate rubbed his forehead. "I didn't realize how much stuff I was going to need." He paid and drove them to his office.

Tate worked on hooking up the computers, personal printers, shredders, and copier. Dani started setting up one room at a time. She stocked the kitchen and bathroom with the items they had purchased at the grocery store. Then, Dani opened all of the office supplies that they'd carried in the night before. She arranged everything the paralegal might need inside her desk drawers. Dani did the same with Tate's desk. She stored the remaining supplies in the bathroom closet. They finally finished with everything at two that afternoon.

Tate and Dani held hands as they strolled through each room. He said, "Thank you so much for helping me. I'm happy with how it all came together."

Dani wrapped her arms around him. "It's the least I could do."

The two drove back to Dani's place and spent the rest of the day relaxing. They walked along the lakefront and lounged on the back porch. At dinner time they ate leftover lasagna and salad in the dining room. Then, they did the few dishes together.

When they finished, Tate sighed. "I hate for this weekend to end, but I need to go back to my place and plan for the week ahead."

Dani smiled. "I had a wonderful time. Thanks for spending it with me."

"My pleasure." Tate gathered the things that he'd brought and loaded them into his backpack.

Dani and Bo walked Tate to the front door. She stood on the porch and waved as he drove away. Dani felt an ache in her heart as she watched him leave.

CHAPTER 13

The next morning, Dani arrived at the office to find Powers sitting at his desk. "Did your doctor say it was okay for you to come back to work?"

"Didn't ask him. I'm feeling better. Anyway, I can't take another day of sitting in my living room watching talk shows and bad reruns."

Dani chuckled as she sat down at her desk. "I don't blame you there."

"Hey, did you hear from Verity this weekend?"

Dani shook her head. She leaned over and placed her handbag in the bottom drawer. "Not a peep. And, I'm happy to say that I didn't even think about him once." She smiled and lowered her voice. "Tate and I spent the weekend together."

Powers arched an eyebrow. "Good for you."

"How's it going with Lucy?"

"Pretty good." Powers grinned. "She's even more commitment phobic than I am."

Dani laughed.

Verity walked into the room. He said to Powers, "Detective. Glad to see you're back and doing well."

Powers nodded and asked, "What's new with Michael?"

Verity sat at his table. "The FBI dug into his past. He's the only child of two very religious parents. They're still alive. Agents interviewed them, but they wouldn't say anything about their son's behavior as a child. He did attend high school with Detective McKenna, as he claimed. The classmates we talked to said he was a loner. It seems that he's a computer expert of some kind. He lives in a condo in Missoula and works from home. The FBI searched his home and car. We didn't find any evidence relating to the women, kidnappings, or torture. Our experts are going through his computer."

Powers frowned. He pushed himself up from his chair. "Wait a minute. You had an FBI team process his condo and car? You know that protocol dictates the same crime scene team should process all the evidence in a case." Powers placed his hands on his hips and shook his head. "What were you thinking?"

Verity stuck his chin out. "At this point it won't make any difference. We caught Michael in the process of killing Ms. Bowers."

Dani tried to break the tension. She asked Verity, "When are you going back to Salt Lake City?"

Verity glared at her. "Are you eager to get rid of me?"

Powers jumped in. "I know I am."

Verity said, "Well, you'll be glad to hear that I'll be gone right after Michael's arraignment."

As if on cue, Connie surged into the room, shoes squeaking. "The initial appearance has been set." Her face was red from exertion as she walked to Powers and handed him the information. She turned and left as quickly as she'd appeared.

Powers sat back down and read from the paper. "Michael's arraignment's been set for tomorrow morning at eight thirty."

Dani asked, "Which deputy county attorney got the case?"

Powers looked at the paper. "They assigned Tiler Keeton as lead and Conrad Noll as co-counsel."

Verity asked, "Are they any good?"

Powers thought for a couple of seconds. "Howland was the best they had. These guys are probably next best."

Verity said, "Normally, we would need to start preparing our testimony. But, Michael confessed. So, the hearing is a formality."

Dani's brow furrowed. Something was nagging at her subconscious, but she couldn't bring it into focus.

Powers saw the look on her face. "What's wrong?"

"I don't know." She shook her head. "Probably nothing." Dani picked up the phone on her desk and called the hospital. When Cindi answered, Dani told her when the initial appearance was to occur.

"What's an initial appearance?"

Dani explained that Michael would be advised of the charges against him and that he would be asked to enter a plea.

"I'm being released from the hospital tomorrow morning. Do you need me to be there?"

"This is just a formality. There's no reason at all for you to attend. Just get well."

"My doctor's releasing me from the hospital tomorrow. I'm going to stay with my parents for a couple of weeks."

"I'm glad. It's good to have the support of loved ones after something like this happens."

Cindi gave Dani her cell number. "Will you call me tomorrow and let me know how it went?"

"Of course. I'll talk to you then."

After Dani hung up, Powers asked, "How's she doing?"

"Amazingly well. Mentally, she's strong. Which is half the battle."

Powers nodded. "Good for her."

Sheriff Tirrell came to the door. He looked at Powers. "Connie told me you were back. Glad to see you're okay."

Powers didn't get up. "Thanks."

Dani didn't miss the fact that Powers hadn't called the sheriff 'sir'.

Tirrell shuffled his feet and mumbled, "Better get back."

When Tirrell was beyond hearing distance, Powers said, "Asshole." He turned toward Dani. "I'm pissed at him for not standing up for you." He turned toward Verity. "When you arrested her for no good reason."

Verity said, "I had a good reason."

Powers shook his head. "You think so? Well, you're an asshole, too."

Dani didn't try to hide the smile that spread across her face.

288

Verity stood and walked out of the room.

Powers said, "I'm not going to miss that guy when he's finally outta here tomorrow."

Dani agreed. She and Powers reviewed the cases that had occurred during the two weeks they'd been working on apprehending Michael. There were two burglaries and one possible arson fire. The two detectives spent the rest of the day driving around interviewing witnesses.

Tate and Dani arranged to have dinner at her house at six. Before Dani left her office, she ordered Chinese food. She stopped on the way home and picked it up. Tate arrived fifteen minutes after Dani. The two took Bo for a walk. The temperature had turned colder and the air smelled of rain, so they opted for eating inside.

Dani swallowed a bite of Kung Pao Chicken and told Tate which deputy attorneys had been assigned to Michael's prosecution.

"They'll do a good job."

Dani eagerly said, "So, tell me about the first day in your new office."

"The first thing I did after I got home last night was consider what area of law I'm going to practice. I know I'm not going to get fortune five hundred corporate clients, and taking any case that walks in the door won't work. So, I decided to stick with criminal defense. It's what I've been specializing in as a prosecutor, and that's where my strengths are. The clientele are individuals who probably haven't worked with a lawyer before. They're looking for someone who cares, who's competent, and who believes in their case."

Dani took a sip of wine. "That sounds like a smart decision to me."

"Serena had all sorts of ideas for how to get started. She developed a list of personal injury attorneys for me to meet with about referrals. I spent most of the day phoning them to schedule a face-to-face. While I did that, she scoured arrest records and developed a list of potential clients. I'm going to the jail tomorrow to meet with them."

Dani leaned back in her chair. "I'm impressed. I wouldn't have had the slightest idea where to start."

"She seems genuinely excited about starting this business with me. Tomorrow she's going to build a website. I hadn't even thought of that. And, I sure don't have a clue how to do it. She said to leave it to her, and she'd take care of it. It'll supposedly be up and running by noon. She's also going to handle the federal and state business licenses and tax stuff."

Dani frowned. "I hadn't considered all the stuff that goes into starting a business... I hope you don't regret your decision to quit and help me."

Tate reached out and took Dani's hand in his. "Not even a little. Please, stop worrying about that."

Dani kissed Tate's cheek.

Tate held onto Dani's hand. "You do realize that my choice of criminal defense means that you and I could be on opposite sides in the future?"

Dani smiled. "I got that right away. And, as you said, please stop worrying about it. We'll work it out."

Tate leaned toward Dani and kissed her. He ended up spending the night. They made love slowly, nearly driving Dani mad with desire.

The next morning, Tate left early. Dani dressed for court. She wore a pair of black trousers, a white button down shirt, and a black blazer.

~~~

The third floor of the Justice Center held the court clerk, the judges' chambers, and the Justice and District Courtrooms. Dani and Powers walked up the two flights of stairs to the assigned courtroom. The detectives moved to the first row behind the prosecuting attorneys. They shook hands all around and took a seat next to Verity.

Dani noted that the room was filled to capacity with spectators, including several members of the press. Dani knew murder sold. Especially when it resembled a horror movie.

The side door of the courtroom opened. Two sheriff's deputies ushered Michael to the defendant's table. He turned to Dani and smiled.

She could feel Powers stiffen beside her. Dani turned her head away from Michael, but she could still see him in her peripheral vision. She took a deep breath to calm her nerves. Dani knew Michael couldn't hurt her, but just having him in the same room made her anxious.

The bailiff walked to the front of the courtroom and stood below the judge's bench. He called the room to order, then said, "The Eleventh District Court of the state of Montana is now in session, the Honorable Judge Adam Stubbs presiding. Please stand." When the judge was seated behind his podium, the bailiff announced the case number and told everyone they could be seated.

Judge Stubbs said, "As required by the state of Montana, I have examined the sworn complaint filed by the Flathead County

Attorney, and have determined that probable cause exists to allow the filing of charges in this case." The judge then informed Michael of his rights, including the right to an attorney and the right to refuse to make a statement.

Michael's attorney stood. He was short and at least fifty pounds overweight. "For the record, your honor, I'm Leonard Keene, acting as attorney for the defendant."

The judge said, "So noted. Have you been given a copy of the charging document, Mr. Keene?"

Keene's brow glistened with perspiration. "We have your honor."

The judge said, "The defendant shall stand and state his true name."

Michael pushed his chair back and stood. "Mr. Michael Gersch, your honor."

The judge read from a document on his podium. "Mr. Michael Gersch, the state of Montana, Flathead County, has charged you with three counts of felony aggravated kidnapping, three counts of felony aggravated assault, three counts of felony aggravated sexual intercourse without consent, two counts of felony deliberate homicide, and one count of felony attempted deliberate homicide. How do you plead?"

Michael said in a confident voice, "Not guilty, your honor."

The entire courtroom began to buzz. Dani and Powers looked at each other. Verity murmured, "What the hell's he playing at?"

Dani closed her eyes. That nagging thing her subconscious had been trying to tell her became crystal clear.

The judge banged his gavel loudly on the podium. "I will have quiet in my courtroom, or all spectators will be removed." He waited for everyone to quiet down. "Mr. Gersch, you may be seated."

Michael sat. He rocked onto the back legs of his chair, smiling like someone who'd eaten his fill and savored every bite.

Judge Stubbs said, "From the information provided by the county attorney, it appears that there is probable cause to believe that an offense has been committed and that the defendant committed it. Therefore, the defendant shall be held for a preliminary hearing."

Keene stood and asked that bail be set at two hundred thousand dollars. The prosecuting attorney stood and began to state his objection.

The judge held up both hands to quiet the two attorneys. "Let me save all of us some time. Bail is denied. Counselors, are there any other motions?"

Both men responded in the negative.

The judge looked at the calendar on his podium. "A preliminary examination for this case shall be held a week from today at eight thirty in the morning in this courtroom." Judge Stubbs banged his gavel down. "Court is adjourned. Bailiff, call the next case."

Verity rushed out of the room and was pacing in front of the courtroom doors when Dani and Powers walked through them. Verity said, "What was that?!"

Dani shook her head. "He never actually confessed."

In a loud voice, Verity exclaimed, "Yes, he did!"

Powers forcedly took Verity's elbow and hustled him down the hall to the staircase. "Hey. There are reporters all around. Let's discuss this in the office."

The three descended the stairs. Powers and Dani kept an unhurried pace down the first-floor hallway. Verity rushed ahead.

Powers closed the office door after himself and said to Verity, "The best way to get unwanted attention is to act upset." Powers swished his hands across the air, like a running news banner. "I can see the headlines now. Lead FBI agent is stunned by not guilty plea."

Verity was clearly agitated. He addressed Dani. "What made you say that Michael didn't confess?"

"It came to me after his plea. Watch the interview again."

Verity pulled up a chair and logged onto the computer on his table. Powers and Dani stood behind him. He tapped keys and found the correct video. Verity started it playing.

Powers hadn't seen the interview before. When the video stopped, he ran his hand over his hair. "Hell. You're right, Dani." Powers walked over to his desk and flopped down onto the chair.

Verity rubbed his forehead, "We'll be called as witnesses at the preliminary hearing, so we better start preparing."

Powers nodded. "Agree. We want the judge to be satisfied that probable cause exists to bind over Michael until trial."

Dani sat down at her desk. "We have two other witnesses that the prosecutor will need to meet with. Bryant Willis and Holly Barton. They can identify Michael."

Powers started counting off on his fingers. "Blood at Cindi's house when I shot Michael. You and Mercer found him standing over Cindi holding a knife." Powers looked at Dani. "Is that the only physical evidence we have so far?"

Dani nodded. "There weren't any fingerprints on any of the notes or photographs. He used a voice changer when he called me, so we can't use voice recognition. We didn't find any evidence in the victim's houses or cars."

Powers said, "We're still waiting for the report from the state crime lab on the cabin. I'll call and tell them we have to have it by Monday at the latest."

Verity said, "I will check on the status of evidence processing from the searches of Michael's house and car."

"We don't have much time," Powers said. "I'll go down and talk to Keene about scheduling prep for witnesses."

Dani said, "I'll get the lineup set." She called Bryant and Holly and scheduled them to come in on Thursday morning at seven thirty. Dani reserved an interview room, then started looking for men similar in appearance to Michael.

Unlike the lineups portrayed in television shows and movies, photographic lineups were used for most suspect identification. Policy prescribed that Dani have five filler photographs for the lineup. All the pictures had to be the same size and have the same background.

Dani took her work camera and the mug shot of Michael down to the jail. She held up her badge to the guard sitting behind a window of bulletproof glass. The guard wrinkled his nose and said, "Weren't you locked up in here a few days ago?"

"Yeah. Case of mistaken identity." Dani shook her head. "Just goes to show it can happen to anyone. Which is actually why I'm here. I need male fillers for a lineup. She pushed Michael's mug shot through the slot in the window. "Got any guys that look like this?"

The guard took the photograph and studied it." Dunno. Maybe. You should probably check for yourself." He pushed a clipboard through the slot. "Gotta sign in."

Dani scribbled her name and slid the clipboard back. A light above the heavy steel door came on, and a buzzer sounded. Dani pulled the door open, stepped into a small entryway, and let the door close behind her. A few minutes later, a male detention officer came to escort Dani. Another light came on above a second door, and they entered the secure area where adults were held. As soon as Dani started walking down the corridor, prisoners started whistling and making catcalls. Dani checked each cell down one side and up the other. There was one prisoner that resembled Michael.

Dani spoke to the officer. He moved toward the inmate's cell and ordered the look-alike to step back. Then, the officer unlocked and opened the door. He told the prisoner to stand against the wall between the cells.

Dani focused the camera on the man's face. He frowned and said, "Hey, what the fuck is this?"

Dani didn't lower the camera. She said, "You're helping out the sheriff's department." Dani clicked the shutter button.

The inmate asked, "WhatdoI get in return?"

Dani smiled and said, "You get to feel warm and fuzzy."

The detention officer motioned for the man to get back inside his cell. The officer locked it behind the prisoner.

The guy turned and said, "Aw, come on blondie. Stay awhile. Let's get to know each other better."

Dani ignored him and the rest of the prisoners that had started yelling. She followed the officer down the hall, out the steel door, and back into the entryway. Dani thanked him and exited the way she'd come. She thanked the guard and walked back down the corridor to the lobby.

Dani climbed the central staircase and started going from office to office, looking inside. She found two deputy county attorneys that resembled Michael. They were both eager to help. Dani had each one take off his jacket and tie, and stand against a blank wall. She had to remind one of them not to smile. She snapped several shots of each.

Dani executed the same search in IT, where she found two more potentials. Their photographs gave her seven fillers. That would allow her to eliminate the one that least resembled Michael.

When Dani got back to her office, she found Powers sitting at his desk. He said, "You, Verity, and I are scheduled to meet with Keeton and Noll at nine Wednesday morning. They'll meet separately with Mercer and our other witnesses."

"Line-up is set for seven thirty on Thursday morning." Dani held up the camera. "I got the fillers." She sat at her computer and opened the department's photo-editing software. Dani connected the digital camera to her computer with the camera's USB cable. She opened the file, set the image size, resolution, and background color, and hit the print command. Dani took ten new manila folders out of her desk drawer. Per the Montana suspect identification policy, six would contain photographs, and four folders would be empty. Dani handed the ten folders to Powers. "Ready for the line-up."

Verity came into the office looking dejected. He waved a thick stack of papers in the air. "No evidence in Michael's house or car. The guy must have removed all of his clothes and changed his shoes before he left his torture chamber."

Dani said, "We've always know he was careful."

Powers rubbed his hair. "Can't say that I'm surprised." Powers was getting ready to say something else when Dani's cell phone rang. She looked at the screen and said, "Hang on a sec." Dani walked out into the hall and answered. "Hey, Garrett."

"Is this a bad time?"

"It's fine," Dani said. "What's up?"

"I have to come to Kalispell tomorrow for a meeting. Can you join me for dinner?"

"That would be great."

"I want to fill you in on a woman I've been seeing." Garrett paused. "Get your opinion."

"Is it serious?"

Garrett said, "I'm hoping it's headed that way."

"She must be special. You usually don't stick around for more than two dates."

"She's pretty awesome."

"I'm intrigued. Can't wait to hear all about her."

"My meeting will probably run late. Can you meet me at the Montana Steakhouse at six?"

"See you then." Dani disconnected and went back inside the office. "What were you going to say?"

"I was going to say that you and I need to go through the Murder Book and double check that everything's in order." Dani and Powers spent the rest of the day studying the information in the six-inch thick binder. Dani hated to admit it to herself, but after the non-stop stress of the last two weeks, she was glad to be doing something more mundane.

~~~

As was becoming their habit, Tate came to Dani's house for dinner that night. There was one Japanese restaurant in Kalispell that had good food. Dani had stopped there on her way home and picked up sushi.

Tate was animated when he arrived. He'd already been retained by two clients, and there was a good possibility for a third. "It's kind of weird to be on the other side," he said as they ate. "Do you know any good investigators? I'm going to occasionally need to hire one."

Dani thought for a few seconds, then shook her head. "No. But, I'll ask around. The guys at work must know someone."

"Thanks." Tate slowly reached out his hand to pet Bo. The dog started growling deep in his chest. Tate quickly withdrew his hand and shrugged. "Thought I'd give it a try."

302

Dani rubbed Bo's silky black ears. "Thanks for being so understanding about him."

"Well, you love him. So, I'll keep trying to get him to like me. Or, at least tolerate me." Tate took Dani's hand in his. "I'm going to miss you tomorrow night. I've gotten used to sleeping next to you." Tate grinned mischievously. "When you let me get some sleep, that is."

Dani almost choked on the wine she was drinking. She laughed. "Is that right? Well, hurry up and eat, and I'll see what I can do to keep you awake again tonight."

Tate jumped up from the table. "I'm finished." He picked Dani up and carried her into the bedroom.

~~~

Wednesday went by in a blur. Dani, Powers, and Verity reviewed the evidence in Michael's case with the two prosecuting attorneys. Step by step, they replayed the timeline. Then, they discussed each time one of them had come in contact with Michael. Dani was the only one of the three investigators that had seen Michael's face, so she would be a key witness.

By the end of the day, Dani had a headache, and she was late for dinner with Garrett. Fortunately, the restaurant was close by, and it only took Dani five minutes to get there. She felt lucky when she found a parking space in the lot of the popular steakhouse. As Dani got out of the Jeep, she tried to remember when the last time was that she'd seen Garrett. Dani smiled and locked the door. She was looking forward to catching up with the only relative in her life.

CHAPTER 14

The next morning, Powers met Bryant and Holly in the lobby and briefly explained the process for the lineup. Powers led them both to the interview room. He asked Holly to take a seat in the hallway and opened the door for Bryant to enter. Verity stood outside of the room, looking in the one-way mirror.

Powers turned on the video recorder in the room. He shuffled the six folders that contained photographs. This was a requirement so that, as the administrator, he wouldn't know the position of Michael's picture. He put the four empty folders underneath the others. This was done so that the witness wouldn't anticipate viewing the last picture. One at a time, Powers handed each folder to Bryant and asked him to look at the photograph inside.

Brant quickly opened the first folder and closed it. He shook his head and held out his hand for the second one. He took the folder from Powers, opened it, shook his head, closed it, and held out his hand for the next folder. After Bryant had looked at all six photographs, Powers said, "The man might not appear exactly as he did when you saw him."

Bryant rolled his eyes. "You said that before. In the lobby. I'm not stupid. But, I'm telling you. None of these are the guy that paid me to deliver that envelope for him. Are you gonna show me another batch of photos?"

Powers shook his head. "No. That's all for today." Powers stood and opened the door. He led Bryant back to the lobby where Ed Abrams was waiting. "Officer Abrams will drive you to school. Thanks for coming in, Bryant. We appreciate it."

Bryant shrugged. "Call me when you want me to come back."

Powers nodded, then went back to the interrogation room. He told Holly he'd be with her in a minute and went inside.

Verity followed Powers into the room, closing the door behind himself. "Well, that was a disaster. Michael's attorney is going do a victory dance when he hears about this."

Powers performed the same folder shuffling as he had previously. He stacked them on top of the table, and said, "He's a young kid. Unreliable." Powers went back to the door, opened it, and motioned for Verity to leave. Powers walked into the hall, smiled at Holly, and asked her to come in.

As he had with Bryant, Powers handed Holly one folder at a time. She picked up the picture in the first folder and studied it. "No. That doesn't look like him." Powers handed her the next file. She examined the photograph inside. Holly set it down, then picked it back up and looked closely at it. "No. That's not him." She did the same with the third, fourth, and fifth pictures. When

Holly got to the sixth one, she spent a few seconds studying it. Then she shook her head. Holly started to pick up the next folder.

"The rest are empty. Protocol." Powers took them all from her.

"Oh." Holly slowly stood up. "It was dark. Maybe I didn't get such a good look at him as I thought."

Powers patted her on the shoulder. "Sometimes we make a line-up without the suspect in it. Also protocol."

Holly nodded. "I see."

Powers walked Holly to the front doors of the Center, then returned to the interview room. Verity was standing inside, pacing. Powers picked up the ten folders. As he walked down the hall to his office, Powers texted Dani. "Problem. Neither witness could identify Michael."

Once they were inside the detectives' office, Verity said, "Shit. Shit. Shit. I'm going to be stationed at Nowhere America if this guy isn't convicted."

Powers brushed past Verity and sat at this desk. "Seriously? That's what you're worried about? You're not concerned that a brutal psychopathic murderer might be let loose to kill more women?" Powers shook his head. "You're an even bigger asshole than I thought."

Powers picked up the phone on his desk and called Dani's cell. No answer. Powers stood up and walked into the hallway and over to Connie. "Did Dani call in sick today?"

Connie shook her head. "I haven't heard from her."

"This isn't like her." Powers stood there, staring at the floor. He looked up suddenly, startling Connie. Powers surged down the hall and back to his office. At Verity's desk, he snatched up the Murder Book. He carried it back to his desk and started flipping through it.

Verity said, "What are you looking for?"

"Wasn't there some unidentified something? Hell, I can't remember what it was."

"A brown hair. Male. In Cindi's car."

"Did we follow up with her? Find out who'd been in her car? Eliminate him?

"I... I don't remember. So much happened. You got shot. Then, we found Cindi."

Powers flipped pages. "Here it is." He read, then started tapping keys on his computer's keyboard.

Verity took the binder off of Powers desk and started skimming the page. "What are you doing?"

"Pulling up the booking photos of Michael." Powers slowly tapped the down arrow key until he came to the one he was looking for. He leaned in closer to the computer's monitor, then said, "No, no, no, no." Powers started clacking keys again.

Verity frowned in confusion. "What? What's happening?"

Powers stopped typing. He picked up the phone on his desk and punched the correct buttons. Powers mumbled, "Come on. Come on." Serena Garber answered. Powers identified himself and told her that it was an emergency. Tate answered seconds later. Powers asked, "Do you know where Dani is?"

Tate said, "She should be at work."

"I'm at the office," Powers said. "She's not here. Did you see her this morning?"

Tate's tone sounded more and more anxious as he spoke. "No. She was having dinner with her stepbrother last night, so I didn't go over to her house." He paused. "Michael's still in jail, right? Right?... Cliff?..."

"There are two of them."

~~~

Dani opened her eyes and blinked several times. When she tried to sit up, she felt dizzy and nauseous. Dani ran her tongue

309

over her dry lips. She rolled onto her side and off of the bed she'd been lying on. The rug beneath her hands and knees was soft. Dani's subconscious kicked in. Loss of consciousness. Difficulty with motor movements. Confusion. Problems seeing... Drugged. She grabbed handfuls of bedding and pulled herself unsteadily to her feet. Dani blinked hard trying to focus. *No. It can't be happening again.* She was inside a cinderblock room with no windows and a steel door.

Unlike the one before, this room was warm and recessed lights bathed it in a bright glow. Dani stumbled as she made her way to an open doorway. She kept one hand on the wall as she entered a small bathroom. A stack of fluffy white towels and washcloths were lying on the floor by the curtainless shower. Sitting next to the sink on the countertop were a few of the same toiletries that Dani used at home. Shampoo, conditioner, liquid soap, and deodorant. All in plastic containers. Dani blinked some more, trying to clear the remaining cloudiness from her vision. She turned on the faucet and ducked her head under it. The water was frigid. Dani drank her fill, then let it run over her face until she felt more alert.

Dani moved back into the main room. She pulled the white down comforter and sheets off of the bed. She saw that two mattresses were stacked on the concrete floor. Dani heaved the top one up on its side and ran her hand under it. She did the same with the bottom mattress. Both were the memory foam kind,

310

without any wire coils. Dani pulled both mattresses back into place and straightened the bedding. She went back into the bathroom, drank some more water, and let it run over her face again.

Dani crossed back through the main room and onto the rug by the bed. She did ten jumping jacks. Then, Dani immediately dropped onto her hands and feet and did ten push-ups. She hopped back up and repeated the jumping jacks. Then, she dropped down and repeated the push-ups. Dani kept doing this repetition until she was sweating and her muscles were warm. She went back into the bathroom and ran more water over her face. Dani wet one of the washcloths and wiped her neck with it. She would have gotten into the shower, but she didn't want to take her clothes off.

~~~

Tate slammed the phone down and ran toward the front door. As he sprinted past, Tate told his paralegal that there was an emergency and he didn't know when he'd be back. The engine of Tate's car raced as he sped the two blocks to the Justice Center. The tires squealed as he slammed on the brakes and parked. He ran down the corridor and into the detectives' office.

Powers was standing next to his desk, talking to someone on the phone. He paced the two steps the phone cord would allow, then back two steps. "See you soon." Powers set the phone back in its cradle. He rubbed his hair. "That was Dani's stepbrother. She never showed for dinner last night. He tried calling her, but she didn't answer. Said he didn't worry about it because he thought she got tied up at work and couldn't call him. He's on his way." Powers paused. "And, just in case, I had the state police go to Dani's parents' house. They haven't seen her and don't know where she is."

Tate's forehead furrowed. "What do we do?"

Verity was sitting at Dani's desk. He said, "This is a police matter, Howland. You don't do anything. You leave it to us."

Tate's clinched his fists and took a step toward Verity. Powers reached out an arm and blocked him. "He's not worth it." Powers turned toward Verity and said, "Get out of Dani's chair, or I'll throw your ass out of it myself."

Verity slowly stood up and stuck out his chin. He turned and strolled out of the room.

Powers said, "Patrol found Dani's Jeep in the parking lot of the restaurant where she was supposed to meet Derrick. It was locked, and the keys weren't in it. No sign of a struggle. She was probably drugged like the three other women. Whoever this other guy is, he destroyed her phone or took the battery out of it. It has a locator that works even when it's turned off."

312

Tate tipped his head back and closed his eyes. His jaw muscles contracted. "What now?"

"I'm going to the jail to talk to Michael. You can come and watch through the one-way."

Tate nodded and said, "Thanks."

Powers led the way down the corridor to the jail. He signed in, and Tate did the same. They were escorted by a guard to the interview room where Michael was waiting. Tate moved to the large mirror to watch. The guard opened the door and entered the room ahead of Powers. He stood against the wall, staring straight ahead.

When Powers entered the room, Michael looked at him with a smug expression. Powers advanced toward Michael. He placed both hands on the table and leaned in. Powers growled, "Where is Detective McKenna?"

Michael smirked. "Detective Powers, how would I know that? I've been locked up in jail."

"Don't even try to feed me that innocent crap. I know you have a partner and I know that he has Dani. Where are they?"

Michael pouted. "How would I know?"

Powers rose up, then slammed both hands on the top of the table. "If anything happens to her, I'll come back to visit you." Powers spun around and stomped out of the room.

Tate hurried to the door. His brow was furrowed, and his eyes looked haunted. "What do we do now? We have to find her."

~~~

Dani walked in circles around the perimeter of the room until she heard the lock of the metal door rattle. She moved to the middle of the room and waited.

The door opened inward and a man entered. Covering his head and neck was a burlap sack with small holes where his eyes and mouth were. His voice was muffled by the mask. "Hello, Justine. I've missed you very much. Have you missed me?"

Dani tried to push down the panic that was threatening to overwhelm her. She stared at the brown eyes behind the holes in the burlap. Dani took a deep breath to calm her nerves. "My name is Dani. Justine doesn't exist."

The man stepped inside, then closed and locked the door. He turned and motioned around the room with his hand. "Do you like what I've done with the place? I did it all for you, Justine. I wanted your home to be better this time. So that you wouldn't want to run away from me again."

Dani shook her head. "I killed the man that kidnapped me. I locked him in. I had the key. He couldn't get out."

"No. You see. When Michael didn't hear from me that evening, he came to see if everything was alright. He had a key. He let me out."

Dani couldn't comprehend what he was saying. "Michael? You and Michael know each other."

"Oh yes. We met in high school. We shared some of the same... shall we say... proclivities. We became good friends because we understood each other." The man walked around the small room, keeping his eyes on Dani. "We always chose the women together. He gets to do his cutting thing with them after I get tired of having sex with them. We shared Josie and Terra that way. But, I refused to share you. So, he got to have Cindi all to himself."

Dani felt nauseous. She concentrated on breathing deeply. In and out. In and out. "You and Michael are partners?"

"I guess you could call us that. The two of us are always together when we take the women. He was with me when I took you the first time, Justine. Every year after you left me, we've shared some women."

Dani tried to keep her tone from sounding as horrified as she felt. "There were others?"

315

"Don't look at me that way. We only took women that didn't deserve to live. We took whores that were selling themselves on the streets." He paused. "But, I missed being with you. I wanted you so much. You were perfect. They weren't."

Dani tried to steer the conversation away from herself. "Which one of you did my partner shoot?"

"That was me. But, it was minor. Just a flesh wound."

"Was it you or Michael that sent the notes and called me on the phone?"

"Michael wrote the notes, and I made the phone calls." The man strolled over to the bed and sat down. "Because I love you so much, Michael felt left out. That's why he went to the press conference. I was furious when he told me that he'd struck you so hard."

Dani tried to sound caring as she said, "You need help. Let me help you."

"Do you mean like putting me in a hospital?"

Dani nodded. "Yes. With a good doctor that could help you."

The man yelled, "No! My father sent me to a shrink when I was young. He figured out that I was the reason our pets kept disappearing." The man stood and held out his hands toward

316

Dani. "But there is a way that you can help me. By loving me, Justine. I love you so much. I've loved you since the first time I saw your beautiful face. You're the only woman I've ever loved."

Dani tried to keep the disgust she was feeling off of her face. "How can I love you when I don't know who you are or what you look like?"

"I'll reveal myself to you after we've spent time together. Getting to know each other again. Making love again. It'll be so much better this time. I've practiced with all those other women so that I could be a good lover to you, Justine. And, I know you've saved yourself all these years for me. When you love me, I'll show you who I am."

Dani's mind whirled as she tried to think of what she should say and how she should act. Nice? Mean? She wasn't sure. But, one thing she did know was that she would never have sex with this man.

"You're very quiet, Justine."

"I'm just a little tired. I'd like to take a shower and freshen up."

"Oh. Of course. I'll leave you alone for a few minutes. But, I'll be back soon. I'm so anxious for us to be together again. I'll make you happy this time."

317

Dani weakly smiled. "I'll be ready soon."

The man moved back to the steel door, unlocked it, and left the room. Dani hurried to the shower and turned the water on. She rushed to the bed and tugged the top sheet from under the comforter. With her front teeth, Dani cut the stitching on one corner. She grabbed opposite sides of the corner and pulled. The sheet started tearing. Dani placed one side under her foot and pulled the other side with both hands. The sheet ripped more. She continued yanking until the sheet was in two pieces. Then, Dani started over, tearing off a strip of material. She ripped the strip in half and stuck one piece in a front pocket of her pants and the other in a back pocket. She threw the rest of the sheet back on the mattress and covered them with the comforter.

Dani rushed toward the steel door. She stood beside it, with her back against the wall. Dani's heart was racing. She took a few shaky breaths. When Dani heard the key rattle in the lock, she pushed herself tighter against the wall. The door swung toward Dani. Through the crack of the open door she could see the man look toward the bathroom doorway.

To be heard over the noise from the running water of the shower, the man yelled, "Justine. I'm back." He paused, listening for a response. "I'll wait on the bed for you." The man took two steps into the room. He must have seen Dani out of the corner of his eye, because he turned toward her and said, "What the...?"

Dani didn't wait for him to finish that thought. She lunged forward, and, using the heal of her hand, hit the man in the nose. Dani could feel the bones break. The man screamed. As he was reaching toward his nose, Dani balled her fist and slugged him in the throat. The man began choking and gagging. He stumbled sideways. Dani bounced off the heel of her left foot, and, with her right foot, kicked the side of the man's knee. She heard a loud pop. The man dropped onto the floor. He writhed around in pain, still wheezing. Dani jumped up and came down on the man's back with both knees. What little air was in his lungs came sputtering out. Dani grabbed the man's broken leg and folded it toward his buttocks. He moaned and attempted to draw air in through his damaged throat. Dani took one of the strips of cloth out of her pocket and tied it around the man's ankle. She pulled his right arm behind him and tied the other end of the cloth to his wrist. Dani used the second strip of material to bind the man's other arm and leg together. He stopped moaning. She could feel the tension leave his body as he lost consciousness. Dani rolled off of his back and knelt on the floor beside him. She jerked the burlap sack over his head. In shock, Dani sat on the floor, staring at her stepbrothers' face.

~~~

Lights flashing and siren blaring, Powers and Tate raced down Highway 93. Tate tapped his foot anxiously on the floorboard. The SUV's tires squealed as Powers made the left turn onto State

Road 82 and again as he turned right onto State Road 35. A cloud of dust followed the vehicle as they drove down dirt roads to the coordinates.

Dani stood in front of an old weathered barn. She could see Powers' vehicle approaching. Before the SUV slid to a complete stop, Tate launched himself out the passenger door. Dani rushed to meet him, throwing her arms around his neck. She held on until Tate took her by the waist and pushed her back. He took Dani's face into his hands. "Let me look at you. Are you okay? Did he hurt you? Are you alright?"

From behind them, Powers said, "Geez, man. Give her a chance to talk, will you?"

Tate and Dani both laughed. Dani moved to Powers and hugged him for the first time. He patted her back and asked, "You okay?"

"I'm fine." She looked back and forth between Powers and Tate. "Honest. He didn't touch me." Dani turned and walked inside the barn doors, then into the cinderblock room within the barn. Powers and Tate followed.

Garrett was still lying on the floor, unconscious. His mouth hung open, and his throat rattled with each shallow breath he took.

Powers walked over to Garrett and stood looking down at him. "I can't believe your stepbrother did all this."

"Believe it. There are pictures on his cell phone." She held it out to Powers. "And, Garrett told me that he and Michael have been killing prostitutes ever since they kidnapped me. Garrett would rape them, and Michael would torture them. Since Garrett wouldn't share me, Michael got to have Cindi all to himself. Which explains why she wasn't raped." Dani shook her head. "Garrett said his father knew he was sick. That's probably the real reason why they didn't call the police. They knew." A tear slid down Dani's cheek.

Tate put his arm around her shoulders and squeezed. "Let's wait outside for the ambulance."

Powers said, "I'll keep an eye on this piece of shit."

Verity arrived before the ambulance. He had, once again, called in the FBI's crime scene to process the barn, and search Garrett's house and car.

Dani, Powers, and Tate left as soon as Verity arrived. Tate sat in the back seat, never taking his hand off of Dani's shoulder. Occasionally, Dani would reach up and rub Tate's hand with her thumb. As they drove back to the Justice Center, she told them the details of what had happened. "I don't remember Garrett grabbing me or drugging me. The last thing I remember is getting out of the Jeep."

Powers told Dani about how he knew there were two perpetrators. "I'm sure the DNA from that unidentified hair will match Garrett's."

Dani shook her head. "I forgot to ask Cindi about that hair."

Tate squeezed her shoulder. "Hey. Don't beat yourself up about that. You couldn't think of everything."

Powers glanced at her. "Yeah. Nobody thought of it. Including that Special FBI asshole."

EPILOGUE

Dani sat in Tate's car, staring at the childhood house that she'd shared with Garrett. She got out of the passenger door and walked up the walkway. She paused a second in front of the door, then rang the bell.

When Dani's mother's opened the door, her face registered shock. "Justine!"

Dani brushed past her mother as she moved into the foyer. "Where is he?"

Dani's mother rushed in front of her. "Justine! Are you okay? They told us you'd been kidnapped again."

With an angry look on his face, Dani's stepfather stepped into the foyer. "What's all the yelling about?" When he saw Dani, he stopped cold.

Dani strode up to her stepfather. Squaring her shoulders, Dani said, "You knew. You knew that Garrett was the person that had kidnapped me. That's why you didn't pay the ransom. That's why you didn't call the police. You didn't want people to know that your son was a monster." Dani glared at her mother, who was now clinging to her husband's arm. "And you! My own mother. How could you?!"

Dani's mother held her hands up to Dani as if in prayer. "You don't understand."

"Really? Well, enlighten me."

Dani's mother looked at her stepfather for help. He said, "We never told you how Damian's mother died." He paused. "Damian loved cars, and she adored him. So, one day she took him out to the forest and let him drive. I was at work, so I didn't know about their outing. Damian was driving when he overcorrected, flipping the car. It rolled down a cliff. My wife was killed instantly. My son had severe head trauma and was in a coma for two days. They kept him in intensive care for two months. He spent two years in therapy learning how to walk and speak again. He always blamed himself for his mother's death. We did what we thought was best."

Dani raised her eyebrows. "Best. Best for who? Your son? Your business. Not for me. That's for sure." She shook her head. "What happened to Garrett is tragic. His becoming a psychopathic rapist is also tragic... for all the women he brutalized." Dani looked back and forth between her mother and step-father." You share some responsibility for their torture and deaths. Because you knew and you did nothing to stop him."

~~~

Even though he pled guilty, Garrett was sentenced to the maximum allowed. He would serve three consecutive one-hundred-year terms for aggravated sexual intercourse without consent, and three consecutive one-hundred-year terms for aggravated kidnapping.

The charges against Michael were amended to three counts of felony aggravated assault, two counts of felony deliberate homicide, and one count of felony attempted deliberate homicide. Within four hours of closing arguments, the jury found Michael guilty of all charges. At sentencing, Judge Stubbs said that if executions in Montana were allowed, he would sentence Michael to death without any hesitation. Barring that, the judge sentenced Michael to be imprisoned in the state prison for three consecutive terms of twenty years for aggravated assault, to be followed by three consecutive one-hundred-year terms for murder.

Dani and Powers were in court every day during the trial and at both men's sentencing. Dani was relieved to know that both men would die in prison. She thought it was better than either of them deserved.

The End

Acknowledgements

I would like to thank you, the reader, for purchasing this book. You make the storytelling worthwhile.

Please take a few minutes to leave a review.

~~~

To contact me directly, email me at: **gillean@gilleancampbell.com**. I would enjoy hearing from you.

You can also:

Visit my website at **https://gilleancampbell.com** and read more about me and how I write.

Follow me on Twitter **https://twitter.com/authorgilleanc** and on

Facebook at **https://www.facebook.com/gilleancampbellauthor/**.

Gillean

About the Author

Even as a small child Gillean was a storyteller. In grade school, classmates would follow her around the school yard as she role played a new story that had come to her. When Gillean's children were grown and she retired, stories started coming to her unbidden. Her problem now is that she can't get the characters to go to sleep at night.

Gillean lives in Santa Fe, New Mexico with her four-legged best friend.